# weirdos

# weirdos

## A NOVEL

### KAT KRUGER

FROM THE FILM DIRECTED
BY BRUCE MCDONALD AND WRITTEN
BY DANIEL MACIVOR

JOE BOOKS LTD

# DREAM ON

ANTIGONISH, NOVA SCOTIA, CANADA

June 30, 1976

**K**it took the steps two at a time. All he could think to do was run. Every beat of his heart pushed a wild mix of emotions into his chest and up into his throat until he had to fight the urge to throw up. He fled to his bedroom, slamming the door behind him and leaning back into it for support.

But neither the hollow-core door nor his wobbly legs were sturdy enough. Sliding down to the carpeted floor, he tried to control deep, shaky breaths, and shut his eyes against the world. In the dark he was still running—still chased by an overheard conversation, by the fragment of a sentence, by a mere word.

He'd gone downstairs to help get snacks ready for movie night with his family, something he did every week. When he'd reached the foot of the stairs, his dad's voice came to him from the kitchen—raised, angry—giving Kit reason to pause. His dad was pretty laid back as far as parents went, but when something really set him off, his temper would flare up. Then the man would try to wash it down with alcohol. That only made things worse. It was a lot better when he just got high.

Creeping quietly through the living room, Kit had listened closely to his dad's rant, which was sprinkled with colourful swears. Kit thought his grandmother was upstairs putting her curlers in, which meant his dad must be talking on the phone. Kit overheard the name of his French teacher at the school where his dad also worked.

Besides English, French was Kit's favourite class and he excelled at it. The other students mostly felt it was a waste of time, particularly because Mr. Bates eschewed teaching Acadian or Québécois dialects and opted for Parisian French instead. Apart from Kit and his girlfriend, Alice, who dreamed of all the far-off places they'd go, the rest of the class never imagined any reason to learn another language because they'd never use it.

"Ignoramuses," Mr. Bates would mutter under his breath.

Among the other teens at school, Kit had developed a reputation for being a brown-noser and an ass-kisser. The innuendo made him uncomfortable, and it didn't stop there. Alice was never subjected to the same kind of name calling. She wasn't popular—not like her sister—but everyone liked her.

"Peter Bates!" his dad had spit out before continuing with a string of words punctuated by a hateful accusation.

Horrified, Kit had backed away and run straight to his bedroom, where he now sat stewing in a mix of helplessness, shame, self-loathing, anger, and something else he couldn't quite put his finger on. If he stood up for Mr. Bates, he'd be cast in the same light. Of that he was sure. Kit knew enough of his peers' circles to know there was a threshold for accepting anything out of the ordinary, a social point of no return in the hierarchy at Antigonish Regional High School. Once an outcast, forever an outcast.

He shifted to get up and call Alice but promptly fell back because he couldn't—his dad was on the phone. That was how all this had started. Besides, then he'd have to explain what he'd heard, and he wasn't precisely sure himself why he was so shaken. Confused would be putting things lightly. What he was sure about was that he couldn't continue living under the same roof as a man who was, Kit decided then, an ignoramus.

"Peter Bates!" his dad had spit out. "To hell with that—"

A bang like a gunshot went off outside. Kit startled. A flash of light outside his window told him it was just early Dominion Day revellers setting off fireworks even though it wasn't completely dark out yet. He suspected it was probably kids in the woods getting drunk and being stupid. Another reminder of why he hated small-town life.

There was no place to hide. Even the forested hangout off the highway was one that everyone knew about. A popular party spot and Kit wanted nothing to do with it. Rumour had it Sue Chisholm got knocked up there last May long weekend. She went to live with relatives for a semester, then came back looking puffy and labelled a slut. And that was that. Once an outcast, always an outcast.

Secrets. Everyone had them. Some people were better at keeping them than others; some secrets were easier to keep. If his dad accused Mr. Bates of—

A knock on the door sent a sensation travelling down his spine and made Kit jump.

"Kit?" his grandmother said. "Are you all right?"

The doorknob twisted above his head and he glanced up at it in panic.

"I'm not decent!" he warned quickly.

"I wasn't about to barge in on you," she said, putting on an affronted tone as the doorknob twisted back into place. "A young man needs his privacy."

He sniffed.

"Are you sure everything's fine?"

"Yeah." He couldn't quite muster a convincing timbre.

"It's soon time for movie night," she reminded him. "Come down and give me a hand with the Jiffy Pop, will you? Lord knows I'll burn it without you, and the kitchen will reek of it for a week."

When it came to cooking, his grandmother was undeniably in charge. She was a bake-sale favourite at church fundraisers, and most dinners would find Kit and his dad looking for second helpings. Yet somehow she couldn't master the art of Jiffy Pop.

"Kit?"

"Sure," he finally answered. If he refused to come down, it would only make things worse. His grandmother would fuss over him and he'd have to fake some kind of illness. Sitting through a movie for a couple hours, even with his dad in the room, would be easier to pull off. "I'll be down in a minute." Then, as the floorboards creaked beneath her shifting weight, he asked, "Can I make a call first?"

"You don't need my permission."

"I know, it's just . . . Dad's on the phone."

She clucked her tongue loud enough that he heard it through the door. "Leave it to your grandmother. Be quick though. It's twenty minutes before showtime and you don't want to miss the opening. We can always make popcorn during the break."

The sound of her footsteps trailed down the stairs, followed shortly after by muffled voices. A few minutes later, Kit's grandmother hollered his name. Standing, he took a moment to compose himself before heading downstairs to the now-empty kitchen. When he picked up the phone and put it to his ear, the low hum of the dial tone marked endless possibilities of people he could call. But there was only one who would understand, who knew what it was like to live in a place that suffocated you—where the whispers of gossipmongers filled the air with toxins, threatening to crush out your life.

He started to dial the rotary. In the morning, he'd fill in Alice.

# LAST SONG

S etting his suitcase on the bed, Kit began to pack the things he'd regret not bringing with him. A muffled voice from the TV downstairs meant his grandmother was watching the morning news. Even after blow-drying his hair, he still had time. After neatly folding a new, wide-collared polka-dot shirt, he stowed it away with other prized possessions: an Edward Bear T-shirt and his favourite pair of runners.

At his bookshelf, he quickly considered what to bring, but the choice was obvious. His hand brushed past Stephen King's *Carrie*, pressed spine-out among dozens of other paperbacks. When Kit pulled down *The Philosophy of Andy Warhol*, somewhere in the back of his head he heard his idol say, "They always say time changes things, but you actually have to change them yourself."

Downstairs, the screen door slammed shut. Moments later, he peered out his bedroom window at his dad, out in the backyard behind the shed and a line of laundry hanging out to dry. With unkempt hair and a shaggy beard, and dressed in a flannel housecoat, the man still had a bit of hippie left in him. Turning toward the house, his dad took a drag off a joint and Kit withdrew from sight.

Promptly shutting his suitcase, he took one last scan of the room. At his shrine to Elton John he pressed two fingers to the temple of the singer's poster-sized image. *Don't let the sun go down on me.* Kit listened at his bedroom door for movement before proceeding into the hallway and taking the stairs down quietly. There were only a few steps between the bottom of the staircase and the front door.

Before bridging the gap, he took a deep breath. In his head, he'd practiced the conversations he might have with his grandmother or dad dozens of times. In these versions, his answers were efficient and nonchalant enough not to raise suspicion—there was no hiding anything in this house. All the same, there were things he wished they would see. The truth existed right under their noses, but they were looking too closely to recognize it. Life under a microscope.

He reached for the knob on the front door. The front entry opened up to a living room that housed an amalgam of formal old and funky new furniture, belonging to his grandmother and dad respectively. A flowery sofa was wedged between large speakers that doubled as end tables. The dulcet tone of a news broadcaster's voice explained, "It's all American, the way we work in various trades, and the ways we worship, the music that makes us sing . . ."

His grandmother waved her hands about in the air to dry her nail polish, fixated on her program. She was a woman who refused to be defined by her age. Other grandmothers he knew wore outdated styles: housedresses or the same style of pants they'd had for generations, the sizes changing every few years. Kit's grandmother, though, would go into the city on shopping trips with him, and he'd help her pick out more fashionable outfits. She loved costume jewellery, and almost always came back with a brightly coloured necklace. Still, she was his grandmother, and had pantyhose with reinforced toes on under her slacks. The necklaces changed, but the hose remained the same.

Kit wore a collared shirt with the top button undone, jeans, and a brown belt that matched his platform shoes—proving that style skipped a generation in his family. He hoped he wasn't trying too hard. Life in a town the size of Antigonish meant he couldn't dress the way he wanted to, like the people he saw in magazines, or how he imagined people dressed in places like New York. His neighbours were always watching, judging. It wouldn't be like that in Sydney.

Kit was going to write the "Great American Novel."
He wanted to be this decade's F. Scott Fitzgerald. Write
what you know—sure—but his life in rural Nova Scotia
was devoid of anything interesting. Kit needed to travel,
meet great minds, maybe even make his way to New York
City one day. First, though, he had to get out of the house.

Just as his hand jiggled the knob of the door, his grandmother spoke without so much as looking at him. "Say
good morning to your grandmother."

Kit set his suitcase down behind the partition wall by
the entrance, hidden from sight. He'd meant to avoid this
conversation. With a weak smile that she couldn't see, he
complied. "Good morning."

"Where are you headed to this early?" She blew on her
fingernails, still watching her show.

"Alice's." It wasn't a lie.

"You've got a jacket?" she asked, turning in her seat to
look at him briefly.

"Yeah." He gestured toward his suitcase, thankful she
couldn't see it. Bringing a jacket now would only mean one
more thing to weigh him down. Besides, he didn't want to
let on that he'd packed for more than an overnight trip.

"It's supposed to rain later on."

He nodded, then blurted, "And I'm staying over."

His grandmother swivelled back, eyebrows raised.
"You're staying the night?"

"Yeah," he replied, kicking himself for having said anything.

"David!" she called out.

"It's no big deal."

It was no use arguing because she hollered again. "Dave!"

His dad ambled in through the back door, holding his big-ass headphones while making his way toward the near-state-of-the-art stereo on the other side of the room. Kit's family went to church on Christmas and Easter but, where his dad was concerned, high fidelity was the altar he truly worshipped at. Especially when he was high.

"Yes, Mother."

"Your son's going out." She sat up primly, pursing her lips.

His dad glanced between them. "Where to?"

"Alice's," she tattled with a knowing nod toward Kit.

More interested in his vinyl, his dad said, "Cool."

"And I'm staying for supper," Kit added again, nonchalant.

"Okay."

"And . . ." his grandmother prodded.

"And staying the night."

His dad looked back at them, so obviously confused about why he'd been called back into the house that all he could do was repeat, "Cool."

"Dave?"

"It's cool," his dad told her.

"He's staying the night."

The way she spoke, it was like code for some nefarious goings-on. Kit had never given them any reason to question him before. In fact, he'd been banking on an easy exit for good behaviour.

"Her mom will be there," his dad said. Then, as if a light bulb had gone off in the attic of his brain he asked Kit, "Val will be there, right?"

"Yeah," he assured them both.

"Mom, it's cool."

Brushing off her defeat, his grandmother grabbed her wallet from the coffee table. "Have you got any money?"

"A little."

The words were barely out of Kit's mouth before she was up and handing him ten dollars. "Always be prepared."

"Mom . . ." Dave balked.

She gave Kit's dad a self-satisfied jut of her chin. Having done her part as guardian, his grandmother made her way into the kitchen. With the interrogation finally over, Kit grabbed his small suitcase and opened the front door.

"See ya," his dad said, leaning down toward the stereo.

In that moment, it struck Kit that this might be the last time he'd see his father, and his dad had no idea. As the man stood flipping through his vinyl collection, a twinge of something pulled at Kit. Suddenly, he was nostalgic for things he would miss when he was gone. Blasting music through the house with his dad while his grandmother was out for tea at a neighbour's. Eating his grandmother's Sunday dinner, with a side of fiddleheads and blueberry grunt for dessert. Lifting weed from his dad's stash and sneaking off into the woods by the highway with Alice. All the little things—the nice things.

Before he left for good, Kit figured he should say something to give his dad one last chance to make things right. Tucking his suitcase behind him, he said, "I think Mr. Bates is an excellent teacher."

"Mr. Bates?" his dad asked, confused.

"My French teacher."

His dad's brow furrowed further as he stepped toward Kit. "Are you having trouble in French?"

Disappointed, Kit shook his head. He couldn't be any clearer. It was a hopeless cause. He made an easy in for his father, held a door wide open, and still, the man would not walk through. He tried to convince himself that there were worse things than not being noticed, than having your feelings negated.

"Okay." For the first time that morning, his dad didn't quite buy it. After a pause, the man prodded, "Everything cool?"

Everything was *not* cool. That was the point. The exact reason he was leaving. Kit's mother understood—would understand. When he'd called her a few days earlier, he didn't explain exactly what had happened. He knew she would get it. She had an artistic temperament. And she knew how stifling this place could be. She'd managed to escape and had even lived in Toronto once.

His dad was born and raised, and would die, in this small town, never knowing what it was like to live beyond the walls he'd put up for himself. It was the thing that had split Kit's parents apart. His dad couldn't hold on to his mom because he didn't understand that she couldn't be changed. She wasn't a puzzle to be solved. She was something else. Like Kit.

Exasperated, Kit walked out and shut the front door behind him. All the time in the world wouldn't change his dad or anything else, so Kit would have to change things himself.

# ROXY ROLLER

**K**it checked the clasps on his suitcase as he made his way down the road toward town. Taking confident strides, he felt light knowing he was about to leave all of it behind—the farmland and rolling fields, and all the old houses on sprawling lawns that had been there since before Kit was born. Where he lived was nothing like Alice's new subdivision, all shiny and new, lined up in neat parcels. But even living in that part of town wouldn't solve the problem.

His freedom, his entire future was with his mother in Sydney. It was a bigger city, sure, but still just a stopping point for Kit. Convincing his mother to move back to Toronto wouldn't take much. For now, her house would be the perfect escape—an artists' commune of sorts, like the way the Factory in New York was a gathering place for Andy Warhol and his friends, true creative types, people of all stripes, and Kit was eager to be accepted there.

The sound of little kids giggling as they ran through a lawn sprinkler in their bathing suits drew Kit's attention for a moment. Just then, Beans rode past Kit on his bicycle. A few years younger, Beans was a pint-sized busybody best ignored. A scrawny kid dressed in a white T-shirt and gym shorts with white gym socks pulled up his skinny calves, Beans's short, blond hair was swept to the side.

"Where are you going?" Beans asked.

"None of your business." Without skipping a beat, Kit continued into town along Main Street.

As eager as he was to get going, he stopped outside the bright window display at Solomon Books. Helium-filled balloons were tied in groupings of red, white, and blue for The American Bicentennial Series by John Jakes. The latest book, *The Furies*, had been published earlier in the summer, and he'd recently borrowed the first book from his dad's shelf. It was a sweeping historical family saga that tied in perfectly with the real-world celebrations that had been ramping up over the course of the weekend. On radios and televisions across the continent, people were tuned in to the bicentennial celebrations for the birth of their nation.

Looking through the store window, Kit was reminded of the kinship he'd felt for some of the characters, especially in light of his own family drama over the past week. He half wished he'd brought more books, but his suitcase was small—lightweight and ideal for his purposes—and he didn't want to draw any more attention to himself than he already had at home.

Taking a shortcut, Kit headed down a wide alley that eventually led to a field and a well-trodden path between spruce trees. When he reached Alice's house, he tucked his suitcase between the bushes out front before entering.

She was in the bathroom packing toiletries into her satchel when her mother yelled, "Alice, Kit's here!"

Alice took one last peek at herself in the mirror before shouldering one strap of her bag. She had on jeans and a T-shirt with the word *Nobody* in felt across her chest. It was worn ironically, daring anyone to notice or comment on it. Denise, the golden child who'd gone to study at Dalhousie University on scholarship, had once owned it, but Alice had swiped it from her suitcase after she'd packed. Denise was the cool one—even from Halifax she shone so brightly that everyone was blind to the existence of Alice.

It surprised no one when her sister decided to stay in Halifax for the summer. People left town and never came back—that's what happened. Denise found a good-paying summer job in Halifax. Their cousin Linda got a job in Moncton at a coffee shop owned by her boyfriend's family. Now Kit was apparently going to live with his mother. Everyone had an excuse to stay away. That's why it was so important for Alice to go with Kit to Sydney. She needed to be the excuse for him to come *back*.

Later that night, they'd be at a party on Dominion Beach, and it would be her last chance to show him they were right together. They'd skipped the party in the woods the night before because hitchhiking to Sydney required a clear head. Plus, it would have made both sets of parents suspicious if they were out after curfew. The plan was carefully made, and even though Kit being with her would probably make it harder to catch a ride, at least they'd have each other's backs if anything went wrong.

She could always count on Kit. He was reliable. It wasn't a bad quality to have in a boyfriend, but it was also a word she could use to describe a favourite piece of furniture. They were too comfortable as friends, yet not comfortable enough as a couple. She wanted that to change this weekend.

When she opened the bathroom door she paused at the sight of her dad as he stopped in the hall on his way past. Dishevelled and half dressed in exactly what he'd been wearing yesterday, it was obvious he'd spent the night again. Now, instead of pants, he had boxers on, and his collared shirt was unbuttoned.

For the past month, he'd been living with her uncle—another reason why Denise didn't want to come home, even for a visit, leaving Alice to deal with the awkwardness of having her dad show up on the weekend, get drunk, and stay the night, like nothing was wrong.

"Alice," he said as if caught, giving her a weak smile.

She was too annoyed to say anything, so he kept moving but turned back briefly to explain. "I slept on the couch."

After taking a second to process the information, she walked down the hall in the opposite direction to meet Kit, who stood by the front door, wedged between the television and stereo. With his hands behind his back, he radiated politeness. Not that he wasn't; he was always nice to her parents. In fact, Alice felt they trusted him more than they did her. Instead of being all the reasons not to let her sleep over at his place, Kit had the opposite effect. Little did they know.

"Are they back together?" he asked in a low voice.

Her parents were on the other side of the partition-wall window, smiling at each other. It was the second time in as many weeks that her dad had stayed the night. Her mom was a bit of a lightweight when it came to booze, laughing more freely after just a single drink, and he'd done a good job of plying her with liquor. Desperate to come home, he was on his very best behaviour, and something was starting to give. After all, her mom hated to be wrong. She'd have to be forgiving him somewhat if she let this keep happening.

Even though it warmed the icy patch that Alice had been trying to form around her parents' failing marriage, she knew it wouldn't last. The weekend before had started off this way. Somehow, her dad would say or do something to set her mom off, and before the day was over he'd be back sleeping at her uncle's place again. Alice was glad that she'd be away and wouldn't have to witness it.

"No," she replied. "He came over for a talk and they got drunk and he stayed. It happens."

"Kit," her dad greeted them as he ambled into the living room and settled onto the couch.

He still hadn't had the foresight to put on pants, and had a beer in hand despite the company and the early hour. Hair of the dog might work for his hangover, but he'd have to work harder on his appearance if he was going to win over her mom.

"I'm going!" Alice announced.

"Kit, she's staying at your house tonight?" Val asked from the kitchen, tapping a cigarette on the edge of an ashtray.

"Yes."

"Is Dave there?" She entered the living room dressed in a cinched-up housecoat and clasping a mug of coffee. "Your grandmother? They haven't gone away or anything?"

"No, Val," Alice answered, squinting in annoyance.

"I'm not Val to you."

"Alice, watch how you talk to your mother," her dad piped up. Alice almost rolled her eyes at his attempt at "parenting."

Just like that, her mom sprang on him like a viper. "Don't get too comfortable."

Taking her words literally, he sat up properly on the

couch while she took a drag of her cigarette.

"Kit, is she smoking?" she asked.

"No." Kit and Alice replied simultaneously.

"I can smell it on you, Alice," her mom remarked with disdain.

"You're smelling yourself!"

That caused her dad to laugh in spite of himself, and he scratched the side of his unkempt hair.

"Does your brother not have a TV?" Val spat out, making him—or at least his expression—sober quickly.

In a soft voice, Alice remarked, "It's nice you stayed over, Dad."

"He slept on the couch," her mom repeated sternly.

Duly reprimanded, her dad nodded in agreement, trying to get back into his wife's good graces. "That's right."

Moving close to Alice so she could get a final word in, her mom whispered, "Don't get your hopes up."

Taking it as their cue to leave, Kit opened the door and walked out with Alice, who riffled through her satchel with a huff. Once they were outside, she lit a cigarette as he snatched his suitcase from the bushes. The awkwardness of Alice's home life hung between them as they walked down the road and made their way out of the suburbs.

Alice let a comfortable silence descend as they walked away from her house. There wasn't much left to say on the matter. Her parents were probably getting divorced.

Alice was glad, in a way, that her dad was out of the house because their fights had escalated from late-night whisper-shouts behind closed doors and sniping at each other over the dinner table to dishes being hurled across the room and screaming matches in the hallway.

The tension was constantly wound tight, like a guitar string, and Alice didn't want to be at home when it finally snapped. Hence, Denise staying away. Hence, Alice getting out as much as possible. The summer days and nights were supposed to be spent lazing about doing nothing around her house—instead, she spent as much time away as her mother would reasonably allow. And Alice, being Alice, pushed her to the limit.

She thought Kit was fortunate his parents had split years ago. He said it was because of his mother's jet-set lifestyle as a model and an artist, which meant that she wasn't around much. She had felt trapped, Kit said. Alice knew it was hard for him because he missed his mother. When he'd called Alice to take her up on the party invitation to Dominion Beach, Kit had also dropped the bomb on her that he was leaving for good. He was following in his mother's footsteps, and complained that she had left because his dad was so small minded. Living with his mom would mean he wouldn't feel like he was on the outside; she would nurture his uniqueness, celebrate that he was different rather than shun him for it.

Maybe it was the quiet between them that drew Kit's attention to the familiar whirring noise of a bicycle chain. He glanced back. Sure enough, Beans was behind them. The boy must have followed Kit into town, unable to resist the chance to stick his nose into someone else's business.

"Are you following me, Beans?"

Instead of answering, the kid asked, "Where are you going?"

"Sydney."

"Yuck. Why?"

"There's a party on Dominion Beach," Alice answered, adding pointedly, "And you're not invited, Beans."

"In Sydney? Gross."

"I'm going to live with my mom."

"Your mom lives in Sydney?"

The way the kid said the city's name sounded like he'd just eaten a lemon, and it turned Kit's mood a bit sour.

"Yes, Beans," he answered in irritation.

"Too bad for her."

Taking Alice's lead, Kit picked up speed in an attempt to get away from the kid. "Yeah, you would think that, Beans, since you're an ignoramus."

"Spaz," Beans said, coming to a stop. He watched the pair stride toward the woods, letting out one last cheap shot before he rode off. "Sydney sucks!"

# GOODBYE YELLOW
# BRICK ROAD

As they walked through the woods toward the highway, Kit and Alice stumbled upon evidence from the party from the other night, broken beer bottles strewn around a burned tire. It was a familiar spot not because of all the parties that took place here—Kit wasn't one for drinking out in the wilderness, considering it too backwoods, both literally and figuratively—but because they came here to smoke his dad's pot sometimes. Somehow that was less provincial.

Stepping around a log by a small pond, Alice tugged at his sleeve, pulling him down with her. She wanted their trip to start out on just the right note. She had it all planned out. Hitchhiking together would be romantic, and then they'd have a rad last day together before finally getting to the beach. Up until now, there was always some reason or other that they couldn't take their relationship to the next level, like the time a few weeks back when they were making out in Kit's room while his grandmother was at bingo and his dad at the Legion.

Alice had wanted them to go all the way then. The moment felt right to her, but Kit pushed back, saying he wasn't feeling what she was feeling. For the number of times he put her off, Alice's stomach always sank. Now that he was planning on leaving, he promised they'd finally have sex, and she was intent on making it happen. Then he wouldn't want to stay away, and Alice wouldn't have to admit how desperate she was for him to stay. He was the one thing that made her life bearable.

Sitting side by side, she leaned in and kissed Kit. They'd made out plenty of times before, but Alice hungered for it now, anticipating the long stretch of time that he'd be away and knowing there was so much more to come before he left. Like all the previous instances, Alice tried to replicate the kisses she'd seen on movies and television, but something was never quite right. It didn't help that Kit kept pulling back, trying to speak—avoiding the intimacy, avoiding her.

"How are you going to get back?" He finally managed to get the words out.

"I told you," she started, smiling at his concern. "I'll hitchhike."

Kit nodded his agreement, but when Alice resumed kissing him, he wouldn't let the conversation go.

"By yourself?" he pressed.

"It's easier that way."

When he bobbed his head again, she went in for another kiss. This time she took it slower, taking a pause to allow him to kiss her back.

"Then maybe I should go by myself," he offered instead, tilting his head as if he'd just asked a question.

Her eyes searched his to determine if he was being serious or if he'd *actually* forgotten about all the things they'd talked about doing before he left.

"What about the party?" Her tone was stern and reminded Alice too much of her mother, so she added lightly, "Aren't we going to the party?"

Because he was insistent on leaving her behind, Alice tried not to anticipate the disappointment that came with his resolve.

"Yeah, we're going to the party," Kit said.

He pecked her on the cheek and got up quickly, picking up a stone from the ground. "Hey," he said with sudden eagerness. "Why don't you take my picture?"

"Why?" There was a laugh in her voice as Alice took the Instamatic camera from her satchel and glanced down at the shutter count.

"It's an important day." Kit hurled the stone into the pond.

"No, I only have two left."

His shoulders slumped. "That's a drag."

As Kit stood in profile, Alice took him in. She wanted to hold on to what they had, but everything was slipping away so quickly. Even Kit himself, who couldn't seem to keep still, not even to kiss. Soon he'd be gone and all they'd have left would be the memories they were still making.

Before him, she'd never kissed a boy. Of all things, it was French class that brought them closer together. It was so cheesy to think back on, she couldn't help but smile. Naturally, they knew each other before then, because every high-school age student in the area went to The Regional. Kit also had the distinction of being the only son of Mr. Morash, the cool social studies teacher.

The other kids were a bit hard on Kit, not just because they expected him to be a nerd, but also because his interests were so far removed from their own. Plus, he tended to dress like he'd just walked out of a fashion magazine. But those were the very things that drew her to Kit: his intellect, his sense of style, his worldliness. He was a bit of a loner. She didn't blame him.

They started hanging out together to study French last semester, and *the* day had started off just like any other session. They'd been preparing for a test on *Le Petit Prince*, sitting outside of class with their backs against a row of lockers, when they both reached for the copy of the book wedged between them at the same time. Their hands brushed, sending a hot rush up Alice's arm. In that moment, toward the end of the school year, it dawned on her that their time together was coming to an end.

"You know," she said, a wistful tone in her voice, "I'm going to miss this."

"What?" He handed her the dog-eared book.

"Studying together," she answered, adding, "Like this, I mean."

He grinned. *"C'est le temps que tu as perdu pour ta rose qui fait ta rose si importante."*

It was a quote from the book, one of her favourite passages. *It's the time you have spent on your rose that makes your rose so important.* Alice took it as a signal and leaned toward him so their shoulders touched, just as voices began to carry down the hall. His eyes flicked past her for just a second and she kissed him. The thrill of being more than just friends mixed with the fear of rejection. When he pressed his lips back against hers that first time, she had smiled. The memory of their first kiss would always be with her.

Since then, all she wanted was to pour everything good she had into their relationship, but instead, she had to show restraint. He always seemed a little bit afraid of what they had, like too much might somehow ruin it. Love didn't work that way. It wasn't like having too much dessert.

Kit told her, again and again, that they were kindred spirits. Alice trusted him when he said they were connected—he wrote stories and she took photos. They appreciated each other's works in ways that no one else could. They were the same in the ways they were different. Different from Denise, different from Mr. Morash, different from her parents, his grandmother. Alice was inspired by his words and appreciated the way he could see the things she tried to capture, how he always noted the lighting or angle or framing of her photographs. They spent their every waking moment together. At school, they sat beside one another in every class. They walked home together. They ate lunch together. They were inseparable. Alice didn't understand how Kit could just leave her behind now. She didn't have another way to fill up the space.

Still, in his writing, though, she could read that he hurt. Deep down, Alice knew it was something fundamental— maybe from his parents' divorce—but his pain stung every page. In a way, she thought her own family situation would bring them closer together. He didn't seem to think it was the same, though, because every time Alice brought it up, Kit insisted his mother was such a free spirit, she simply couldn't be confined by marriage.

"Are we going to have goodbye sex?" she blurted, suddenly not caring how desperate it made her sound.

"Yes," he assured her, moving back toward the log to bridge the distance between them.

"When?"

"When we get there, Alice. Like I said."

"So then I guess that means I'm going with you, aren't I?" she said, putting on an air of confidence, grinning.

"Yeah," he agreed.

Kit looked away but not before she snapped a picture.

"Hey!" he balked. "I wasn't ready!"

Alice laughed. "It's better that way."

Rather than argue and risk ruining the mood, he threw another stone into the pond. Alice kept smiling. Soon, they'd know what it would be like to experience one of those off-camera love scenes. She stowed the Instamatic and with it the frozen-in-time moment that would be the last picture of Kit before they finally made love.

# SIGNS

**K**it and Alice walked along the gravel shoulder that edged the road leading toward a highway underpass. He was looking forward to living in a city with proper sidewalks everywhere instead of kicking up gravel and having dust collect on his shoes. A light breeze billowed through a windsock and undulated tall wheat as a tractor collecting bales of hay rumbled along a field. The cool wind was a kind reprieve from the summer heat.

"Hey, maybe we should go up there," she suggested with a feeble gesture toward the ramp. When he didn't answer, Alice skipped ahead. "I'm going to go check it out."

Lost in his thoughts, Kit fell back as she made her way up the hill. Leaning into a concrete pillar with an old graffiti of a cartoon face, he wondered what Andy Warhol would say about all of this.

*You're going to wreck those shoes*, he imagined.

Then, there he was—wearing a platinum wig, black turtle-neck, and square-framed glasses. He stood with one hand propping an elbow, fingers to the side of his jaw, as if waiting for a cigarette to appear out of thin air, just as he had.

Taken aback, Kit glanced around to see if anyone was around to witness his imagination come to life. "Are you Andy Warhol?"

"No," the imagining replied in a blasé manner. "I'm just a guy in a wig."

"What are you doing here?"

Andy Warhol glanced up at the sky as if to pluck an answer from above. "I'm your spirit animal. Do you know what that is?"

With a shake of his head, Kit said, "No."

"I read about it somewhere. I think you can ask me anything."

"Like what?"

After mulling over it for a long while, Andy Warhol decided on an appropriate response. "Anything, I guess."

Kit sighed, brow furrowed with concern. "Am I doing the right thing?"

"I don't know," Andy Warhol answered, so quick it was almost flippant. "What do you want?"

"I want . . ." Kit's eyes wandered up toward Alice, who had just reached the top of the ramp. "I want things to change."

"Is that possible?"

"I guess."

"It's always better if people only want what's possible."

The idea rattled Kit's head. "How does someone know what's possible?"

"Anything's possible."

"So someone can want anything?"

"No," Andy Warhol asserted. "Just what's possible."

Kit was utterly confused. "Oh."

"But I do know that things don't change on their own." Andy Warhol stared off for a spell before suddenly noticing Alice. "Is that your girlfriend?"

"Yeah."

Andy Warhol titled head his head to fully assess her. "She looks a little butch."

"You're going to ruin those shoes," Alice called down.

Climbing up after her, Kit left behind his imagined conversation. He took care to not scuff his platform shoes on the concrete embankment beneath the overpass before trudging into the grass.

"Come on," Alice urged him along. "Hurry up."

When they crested the top of the hill, a long expanse of highway absent of any cars stretched out before them. They continued to walk. Kit picked up a big stick along the way and swished it through the tall grass with one hand, his suitcase heavy in the other.

Kit's throat was dry. He'd never hitchhiked before, and only now realized that he hadn't thought to bring anything to eat or drink. He wished he had packed an apple, stashed one of his grandmother's day-old scones, or even had a spare stick of gum in his pocket. All he wanted was to get away. He hadn't even thought to ask Alice any questions about what hitching was like because he trusted her just to know. With the combination of sweat and dust gathering on his skin, he'd look like a streel by the time they got to the party.

Meanwhile, Alice talked about a new song she'd heard on the radio. Her own parents only ever listened to the CBC, but sometimes she'd tune in to CFXU-FM "the Fox," the campus radio station out of St. Francis Xavier University.

"Does your dad have any new music?"

When Kit didn't respond, she turned back to see he'd fallen behind. Slowing her pace, Alice realized she probably should have told him to at least wear comfortable shoes. They might have to walk a fair bit. Hitchhiking was like panhandling, and some days there were long stretches of sifting through time before striking gold.

"So, like, how long will it take to get to Sydney?" he asked.

She was walking ahead of him and turned around to answer, taking measured steps backward as she spoke.

"If we're good at it and get a ride through, it's about two hours," she started, "but if we're stunned it'll take us till tonight."

"Tonight?"

"Well, it's up to us if we're stunned or not. There's a way to do it." She stabbed a finger at him. "With a suitcase, even a small one like that, you want to stand in front so they can't see it."

When it came to hitchhiking, she was hands down the expert. He did as he was told, setting his suitcase down and positioning himself in front of it.

"And you want to look like you don't really need a ride," she added, moving spryly in one place like her bones were made of jelly. "Like it's no big deal. Look like you do this all the time. Sort of bored."

Watching her, Kit wasn't sure he could pull it off. It *was* a big deal—to him at least. Leaving this town behind so he could live with his mother was the biggest deal of his entire life. On the phone with her earlier in the week, the conversation had started off without any expectation, he'd simply called to hear her voice and to talk with someone who'd understand what he was going through.

He'd recently gotten his hands on the latest issue of *Interview* magazine. Solomon Books brought the magazine in on special order for him, and even though it always arrived late in the month, he'd pour through the pages and reread it until the next issue came in. By then some-times the pages would have fallen out from being flipped through so frequently.

He only knew about the magazine because of his mother, having been gifted a copy on one of his visits to see her. It was the February 1972 issue with Marilyn Monroe on the cover, and when he told her about finding it recently, she'd laughed and then done her best rendition of "Happy Birthday, Mr. President" over the phone.

The latest issue featured an interview with Dustin Hoff-man, who played one of the leads in *All the President's Men*. Kit was in awe of all the interesting people Andy Warhol crossed paths with while living in New York. As was often the case, the conversation was recorded over dinner at the Quo Vadis restaurant, and as a result, the actor had commented on Andy Warhol's metabolism.

Kit had mentioned the article to his mother during their call earlier in the week, " . . . Dustin Hoffman said, 'You must burn it off with all your angst.' And Andy Warhol said, 'No, I wear a corset.'"

They had cracked up over the quirky response. It was good to hear his mother's laugh, how unburdened from the weight of the world she was.

"Does he really wear one?" he had asked.

She'd met Andy Warhol once in Toronto. Kit never grew tired of hearing that story.

"*C'est très impoli*!" she'd exclaimed in a teasing tone. "One doesn't ask such things."

How could he ever be expected to know what was a social faux pas when he lived in the middle of nowhere and his experiences would forever be limited to listening to his grandmother lecture his father about falling asleep on the couch and getting Cheezies crumbs on the cushions? His mother had seen so much of the world. His father hadn't. Kit longed for the knowledge and freedom that came with living his mother's bohemian lifestyle.

"Mom, I don't want to live here anymore," he blurted. "I can't."

"Oh, baby," she cooed. "Honey."

When she let out a sigh, he knew there was nothing she could do, nothing he could ask her to do. And in the long silence after, he considered his options. Maybe he could make it to New York on his own.

And then she'd said, "Come and stay with me."

"When?"

"Anytime, lovely. For lunch, for supper, forever."

She'd hung up the phone then, disappearing again, before Kit could answer yes, yes, he would like to come and stay. Yes, he needed it, needed her, now more than ever.

A car approached and Kit tried to incorporate all of Alice's suggestions into his stance, channelling his most aloof self. He stuck out his thumb and Alice instantly slapped his arm down, prompting him to turn to her in disbelief.

"Hang on," she instructed, staring down the road at the oncoming vehicle. "You don't thumb for every car. You have to check it out first."

"Check what out?"

"No old guys alone." As she kicked the toes of her runners on the gravel, Alice spotted the driver. "Old guy alone. Walk on."

She turned in an instant, striding away with her head held high. Kit picked up his suitcase and followed, letting the car pass. Moments later, they heard another vehicle approach. Alice assessed the situation.

"Oh, okay," she said. Then added, pointedly, "And be cool."

When she stuck her thumb out, he let out a sigh and mimicked her. While he was casually smoothing down his hair with his free hand, the car drove by without so much as slowing.

"Looks like you weren't cool enough," Kit remarked.

Ignoring his sarcasm, Alice threw back her head, shoulders slumping in frustration. They walked along the highway, having no choice but to carry on, crossing a bridge spanning a picturesque river. In the summer, the water took on a deep-blue hue and the sun cast diamonds on the surface. Alice had taken a dozen photos in an attempt to capture it, but they were never quite right when she developed the film.

From this elevated angle, Kit didn't recognize the river at first, but as they walked over the bridge, it brought back a childhood memory of a summer day like this when he was just a little boy and his parents were still together. His father was trying to teach him how to fish while his mother sunbathed on the rocks. She was wearing a wide-brimmed, white straw hat and a high-waisted floral bikini. A car horn honked from the bridge above and Kit, who was only six at the time, had thought someone recognized her from a magazine.

His dad remarked lightly, "You're going to cause a car wreck."

To which she simply smiled, tilted her head back, and closed her eyes. Kit didn't realize it at the time, but that day was an escape, a mirage, and he'd been trying to find that happy family balance with his dad ever since his mother left the winter after that day. Everything about this trip was to prove to his father they could never understand one another. Now Kit needed to be with the parent who could understand him, way deep down where it mattered.

Alice tried to hitch a ride every so often, but the drivers who did pass weren't interested in picking them up. When they had talked about hitchhiking to Sydney for the party, she had told Kit to pack light. She didn't expect him to show up with a suitcase. Somehow, the very shape of it made his going away more real. The luggage kept staring her in the face, challenging her to find a way to unburden him of it. Hurling it into the woods would be too obvious.

When they stopped for a rest, Kit sat on his upright suitcase and grabbed a handful of gravel in the palm of his hand. "Do you think some people are 'lucky' and some people are 'not lucky,' or do you think that some people are 'lucky' and everybody else is just 'regular'?"

Alice stood waiting for a car, considering the theory. "I don't know."

Tossing a small pebble onto the road, Kit said, "I think some people are 'not lucky.'"

Hooking her thumbs onto the straps of her satchel, she let the idea settle. Like her shirt said, she was a "nobody," and after fifteen years of being that way, she didn't know how to be anything but that. Luck was something that happened to other people, like her sister, and maybe there was only a finite amount of it to go around in each family. There simply wasn't enough luck in the world to spread around.

Denise had received a scholarship to study at Dalhousie, and it seemed to Alice that her sister had a free pass on life, too. It had been that way always, and there were no signs of it coming to an end. Denise had even landed a summer research position at the university, which accounted for why she didn't have to come home after the semester ended and face their family drama. To top it all off, she was also pretty in a classic sort of way. Alice had lost count of all the boys at school who still pined over Denise even after she'd been gone for the whole school year.

The distinct sound of a car approaching drew her attention. Without thinking, Alice thrust her thumb out. As the vehicle got closer, she put her other arm up to shield her eyes from the sun and take a better look. Suddenly she began yelling and waving her arms, jumping up and down on the side of the road.

"I thought you said to be cool," Kit reminded her.

"I know them!"

As the vehicle came closer, someone waved back from the passenger seat. The driver honked before slowing down and pulling over for them.

"Lucky!" Alice yelled, running ahead. "Come on!"

Picking up his suitcase, Kit raced her to the car. Finally, he was on his way.

# OH, WHAT A FEELING

Soon, Kit found himself crammed into the back of a Pontiac with two other boys. The one closest to him had his arm stretched along the top of the seat. His wavy hair was tousled and his face radiated with welcome at the surprise of finding Kit on the side of the road. They smiled timidly at each other as Kit set his suitcase on his lap while Alice crowded in next to him.

As the driver pulled back onto the highway he made introductions. "That's Nalin and Marylou and Jeanie."

He pointed respectively to the boy by the back window and two girls up front, a brunette and a blonde.

"Alice is Denise's sister," he announced to everyone.

"Denise Keating?" Jeanie, the blonde, asked with disdain.

"Yeah," Alice answered, hating the fact that she was always introduced by way of her sister.

"And that's Leo," the driver added. "Jeanie's brother."

"Yeah, I know Leo," Kit said at almost the same moment Leo said, "I know Kit."

Each of them smiled again, but neither made eye contact this time.

"I'm Jack," the driver rounded out his introductions.

"Mr. Morash is Kit's dad," Alice declared, knowing the cachet the Morash name carried with the in-crowd.

As if to take stock of Kit and confirm any resemblances, Nalin leaned forward. "Is Mr. Morash your *dad*?"

"Yeah."

"Mr. Morash is super cool," the driver commented, causing Alice to smile at Kit.

"Who's Mr. Morash?" Marylou asked.

"Mr. More-Hash, nimrod," Nalin told her. "Social studies. Jeez."

"Shut up, Nalin."

Leo gestured to Kit's lap. "I like your suitcase."

"Thanks."

Taking notice, Jack asked, "So why are you going to Sydney?"

Kit was so happy to answer that he failed to notice Alice willing him not to say anything. "I'm going—"

"—There's a party on Dominion Beach," she cut him off.

"No way! Let's go!" Nalin suggested, much to Alice's chagrin, and she regretted telling them about the party almost immediately. She had wanted to be anonymous in the crowd and had expected to have Kit to herself—it was going to be hard enough to pull Kit away at the beach, and having a bunch of tagalongs wasn't a part of the plan. Even though she didn't want to believe Kit was going for good, this road trip was supposed to be special—just the two of them together, taking their relationship to the next level.

"Are you going to the party?" Leo asked him.

"Probably," Kit answered meekly, then more definitively, "Yeah."

"Let's all go to the party!" the boy exclaimed.

Kit had never been one for parties, but somehow he got caught up in Leo's excitement—a real summer experience, something to tell his mother about the morning after. Mothers and sons who were close had those kinds of intimate conversations. Or so he imagined. Half gossip, half truth. His mother could tell him more about her wild days in Toronto . . . Kit drifted off into the imagined scenario as everyone talked at once, excited about the prospect of a beach party. He didn't notice Alice go quiet in the seat beside him. Disheartened at the turn of events, she looked over for Kit to commiserate in silence with her, but he was so oblivious to her misery that he actually mouthed the word *Lucky*.

Music blared on the radio as they sped along the highway and random conversations floated around the car. While the two girls up front talked about a beer run, Nalin picked up a Super 8 camera and started recording. Alice shrunk into her seat—she just wanted a ride, not all this. Kit had barely looked at her since they got into the car, and instead kept smiling over at Leo, like he was Kit's new best friend.

After what felt like an eternity to Alice, Jack turned down a stretch of dirt road. Up ahead was a rundown, old house, with the siding stripped off and a ladder leaning up against the front. A Canadian flag covered a lone window from the inside. Nailed against torn plastic weather sheeting was a sign that read *Private Property*.

"Who lives here?" Alice asked.

"The bootlegger," Jack announced with fanfare in his voice.

They parked out front and Marylou exited the car, scurrying up to the shack. Alice pictured a toothless old man inside with nothing but overalls and a shotgun.

"I'm actually going to live with my mom in Sydney," Kit said to Leo, aching to tell him more.

She wished he would stop going on about moving away. It felt like such a lie.

"Where's your dad?" Leo asked.

"Home."

"Why's your mom in Sydney?"

"They're divorced."

"Cool," he said, then to Alice, "So how's Denise doing at Dal?"

"I don't know," she answered, tired of the same old question. "Good, I guess."

Jeanie turned so Alice could get a clear look of her pretty profile without making eye contact. "Is she still a snob?"

Even though Alice disliked the near obsession everyone seemed to have with her sister, she wasn't about to let the comment slide. "Denise isn't a snob."

"Yeah. *Sure.*"

"She's just a nerd that doesn't know it yet," Alice added, smirking at her own wisdom.

Nalin peered over at her again. "Is she really going to be a doctor?"

"I don't know. I guess."

"That's weird," he remarked.

"Why is that weird?" Jeanie asked.

"It's just weird."

"Shut up, Nalin."

Alice had to give Jeanie some credit. At least she distributed her bitchiness evenly.

"I gotta take a whiz," he announced, getting out of the car and leaving his camera with Leo, who turned it around in his hands like it was alien space debris.

"Pass the camera." Alice snatched the Super 8 from him and opened the back door, hoping Kit would ask where she was going. He didn't.

Instead of looking up at her, he asked Leo, "You want to see something cool?"

"Sure."

Kit unlocked his suitcase and pulled out the latest edition of *Interview*. Annoyed, Alice slammed the door. In the front seat, Jeanie got cozy with Jack as Alice walked to front of the car and leaned against the hood.

With the Super 8 in hand, Alice took in her surroundings. The rundown house was situated in a clearing on the edge of a forest. She figured if the cops came, the bootlegger inside could see them coming and head for the woods. A fleeting wish for the police to show up overcame her. Not just for the excitement, but because that's what it would take to pry Kit away from his new friend.

She kept recording. Tall weeds intermingled with the yellowed grass, highlighting the lack of any yard maintenance. Behind her, Nalin stood only a few metres away from the car, the front of his pants unbuttoned. She panned the camera away. On a beer run at some crazy old bootlegger's shack in the middle of the woods was the last place she imagined she'd be today. Alice had thought she'd have Kit to herself for most of the day, giving her time to coax him toward the moment they would make love. Sure, getting a little drunk at the beach party was in the cards, if anything to take the edge off, which Kit needed more than she did. He was so tightly wound up about sex that he kept putting it off. But once they got to their destination, there'd be no more excuses.

She had heard of the party at Dominion Beach through her cousin Terry, who could no longer go because she'd been grounded. At the time, Alice had thought it was just as well because she didn't want to deal with having a third wheel around. What Alice had envisioned was drinking some of the lemon gin she'd brought, then taking Kit by the hand and walking to a secluded spot on the beach where they'd make out and finally do it. That moment was supposed to be teased out over the course of the day. And when it happened—when they connected so intimately— he would see how foolish it was to think they could live apart from each other. Maybe he had put it off for so long because wanted their first time to be perfect, and she had to admit that doing it under the stars by the ocean would be romantic.

Alice hadn't really expected Kit would let her hitchhike all the way back to Antigonish on her own. The trouble was, the more time he spent with people who supported his belief that he was going to live with his mother, the more real it would become. Kit actually seemed serious about it, and if he went through with it, he'd break her heart. Lost in her thoughts, Alice didn't notice the car door slam, but as Jack sidled up next to her, she felt the weight of him shift the metal hood beneath her.

"So why's his mom live in Sydney?" he asked, muscles flexing as he crossed his arms.

"He's not actually going to live there," she confided, shaking her head at Kit's unrealistic ambition. "He just says that."

"His dad is super cool."

With a nod she said, "Yeah, he's okay."

Jack put his hands down on either side of him, clutching the hood of the car. "What's his mom like?"

"I never met her."

"You never met his mom?"

"I saw pictures though." Her voice took on a dreamy quality to it as she recalled the images Kit had shown her. "She's really beautiful. She used to be a model. But he's not going to live there. He's just going to visit."

"Cool."

Marylou appeared at the door of the shack, waving desperately as she called out, "I need five more bucks!"

"Oh, for frig's sake!" Jeanie muttered, getting out of the car and running over with the extra cash.

Leaning closer to Alice, Jack noted, "Jeanie's not my girlfriend."

It was impossible for her to hide her surprise as she glanced over at him; all the same, she tried to suppress a smile, but he stared down at her.

"Oh," she said, swallowing back her nerves and playing it cool. "Okay."

He pushed off the hood, looking back at her to ensure his meaning was clear before sprinting toward the shack. Once he was inside, her eyebrows furrowed as she tried to figure out what to do with that information. Maybe she should have told him that Kit was her boyfriend.

Laughter came from the car just then. Turning back from where she stood, Alice stared through the windshield, willing Kit to acknowledge she even existed. But he was too deep in conversation with Leo to even realize another boy had just come on to her.

Alice caught snippets of what he was saying. The only subject matter that ever got Kit this animated was Andy Warhol. He could talk about the man for hours—how cool and weird and amazing a complete stranger was. And Leo was just soaking it all in.

He was talking about that strange movie, *Empire*. It was just eight hours of nonstop, slow-motion footage of the Empire State Building in New York. What was so interesting about that? Alice could do better. Instead of resigning herself to being an uninteresting nobody, she held up the camera and started filming her surroundings.

But no matter how long she recorded the woods and the ramshackle house, she couldn't escape the feeling of being the unluckiest girl in the world.

# SOMETHING FOR NOTHING

Alice's dad peered into Kit's house through the screen door, squinting as if to see past the music blasting from within. He stood on the porch and knocked a few times, increasingly vexed by the lack of response.

He'd needed to get out of the house for a bit to give his wife some time to sleep off her hangover, and had figured that Dave Morash was always good for a beer. Other things, too, but Joe never touched that stuff.

At the first sign of movement from within, he was quick to put on a smile that turned into a wry grin when Dave appeared. The man's eyes were glazed over as he held the door open with one hand, clutching a bag of Cheezies in the other. Little orange crumbs were stuck in his beard.

"Hey, Joe."

"You look like you have the munchies," he remarked with a laugh in his voice.

As if only then realizing he was holding the bag, Dave said, "Right." He gestured inside. "You want a beer?"

"I never say no."

They made their way into the kitchen, Dave setting down the Cheezies on the kitchen table by the lit joint in an ashtray. He cracked open a cold beer and handed it to Joe before picking up his joint and leaning against the counter.

Planting himself on a painted wooden chair, Joe lit a cigarette. The kitchen had a woman's touch. Dave's mother, Mrs. Morash, clearly kept a tidy house. Joe had been living long enough at his brother's place to recognize the little things—the placemats on a flowery tablecloth, a sink clear of dishes, and even the scent of Palmolive dish soap that managed to linger in the air despite the odour of marijuana.

"Are you still living with your brother?" Dave asked.

Joe took a drag before answering. "Not for long."

Maybe because Dave didn't pursue it or maybe because Joe just needed to convince himself, he added, "I'm really starting to wear Val down."

"Wasn't that the problem in the first place?"

"No, the problem in the first place was that I didn't appreciate her."

"And now you do," Dave said with a smirk, tapping ashes into the sink behind him.

"After living with my brother for a month? Oh, yeah. My brother, he's a single guy. Not me. I'm not built for that."

"Some of us don't have a choice."

Even though Dave said the words lightly, they weighed heavily on Joe, who let everything sink in to his very core. It was a sad state, a single man raising a kid on his own, having to move back in with his mother. Dave had had it good once. Nice little house. Beautiful wife. Polite kid. But Joe knew too well how the saying went: *all good things . . .*

"How's Laura doing?"

The former Mrs. Morash had been the talk of the town while she was still married and living in Antigonish. A rose among wildflowers. Too bad about the thorns.

"Apparently she moved into a new place."

Smoke blew out of Dave's nostrils as he spoke. His ex-wife had always been a hard one to keep tabs on even when they were married and living together. In between the times when she was away, she'd still need space. "To think, to breathe, to live, to thrive," she would say. Then she would disappear, only calling or checking in when it suited her.

Dave sometimes worried that Kit had a little of his mother in him, the way he'd shut himself away to write. That's why he was so glad for Alice and the time she and

Kit spent together. A few youthful indiscretions were exactly what his son needed—life outside his own head. At fifteen, Dave had experienced many firsts: first kiss, first joint, first time getting laid. Rites of passage. That's all he wanted for Kit—a normal, lived-in life that he wouldn't get sitting in his bedroom writing stories all day.

"Pity about all that," Joe remarked, casting a sympathetic glance Dave's way. "Still, have to admit you had some good times."

"That we did."

Catching himself in a memory, Joe shook his head. "The two of you would throw some great shindigs back in the day. Don't get me wrong—I mean, Laura couldn't fire up a scoff to save her life, but she sure knew how to entertain!"

"She made fondues."

"That's uppity talk for boiled cheese! It'd sit like a brick in my gut for days."

Dave chuckled. "Maybe you shouldn't have eaten so much of it."

With a pat of his belly, Joe agreed. "Always been my problem. Nevertheless, we always had a time at those parties, me and Val. One thing Laura was always good at was charades."

"She *was* a theatre major when we met."

"You could have taken some pointers from her."

"You're one to talk!" Dave ribbed back, good naturedly.

"What are you on about?"

Instead of answering, Dave shook his head and left Joe to come to his own conclusion.

"What, you mean that one time? For the life of me, I still don't know what she got so worked up about."

The incident in question had taken place over a decade ago, when Kit and Alice were just learning to walk. It was at one of the parties at Dave's old place on the other side of town. After the fondue pot had been scraped clean and not a piece of bread was to be found, they got around to playing charades. Enough drinks had been imbibed to loosen up the few among them who were a little self-conscious about the game.

"You have to admit, it looked just like Marilyn Monroe," Joe still asserted.

"It was the Eiffel Tower!"

Joe recreated what he believed had been Laura's pantomime, indicating an exaggerated hourglass. "Tell me what that was supposed to be."

"She said the clue was an *object*," Dave reminded him.

"Exactly!" Joe said, as though they were in agreement. "What's more, there was no need for name calling."

While Dave couldn't blame his wife at the time for being angry, he also knew his friend would likely go to the grave without ever knowing why Laura Morash called him a Neanderthal that night. Even all these years later, with two nearly full-grown daughters, Joe couldn't wrap his brain around it.

"And afterward, she didn't figure out my clue on purpose."

"I doubt that," Dave said. "Laura doesn't like to lose."

"Well, how else do you explain it? For Christ's sake, it was a cradle. Any woman with a maternal instinct—"

It was then that Joe cut himself off, knowing he'd gone too far. Some old wounds were best left in the past. Truth was, all those parties back in the day only happened when Laura was in town. And after Kit was born, that was less and less often.

When Joe's turn had come around, he had tried to mime "cradle," thinking it was an easy one. Laura had failed to guess the right answer, then had accused him of being a poor sport for not putting effort into it. Compounding the tension, Val, in an unusual act of support for her husband, had sniped, "What would you know about babies?"

In an attempt to make up for having put his foot in it now, Joe said, "Maybe you didn't have a choice, but in the end, it's for the best."

Staring off at nothing, Dave merely murmured in acknowledgement. Joe swigged his drink quietly until he finished it, more determined than ever to make things right with his wife.

"Thanks for the beer."

"Yeah," Dave responded absently as he played with a matchbook.

Joe got up to show himself out but stopped himself. "Actually, it's great Alice is sleeping over tonight," he said with a smile. "One more night to work my magic on Val. And if the magic doesn't work, I'm going to start begging. Where are they?"

Dave stopped what he was doing and stepped away from the counter. "What?"

"Where's Alice and Kit?"

It was a simple enough question, one that Dave might have asked if the roles had been reversed that afternoon and he'd gone over to the Keatings' place for a beer instead. Connections slowly formed in his brain.

"Out," he said, adding a smile for reassurance.

"Right. *Out*," Joe repeated, anything but reassured. At least he knew that Dave's mother would be around to look in on the kids. "Thanks for the beer."

Dave leaned his arm against the top of the fridge as if to support himself. "Yeah."

Leaving Dave standing in the kitchen seemingly staring off in a daze, Joe drove back home. But when he heard the car rumble away, Dave picked up his keys.

Kit was a good kid. Of course, Dave had no illusions that his son was without fault. He knew Kit got up to a reasonable amount of trouble, but nothing that Dave hadn't done himself at that age. When Kit would come home a little drunk or high, Dave pretended not to notice. For his son to outright lie about where he was staying the night meant he was hiding something big. Every scenario ran through his head—Kit taking off for Toronto, Kit and Alice in real trouble, Kit dead in a ditch, Kit heading somewhere away from him, forever.

A million thoughts raced through his mind, one more troubling than all the rest. He hoped to God it wasn't that. Pushing down his fear, Dave Morash took off in search of his son.

The last time Kit had run away from home was right after Laura had left. Although Kit had only made it across the field given he was just a little boy at the time, Dave still felt the sting of the day intensely.

# GOT TO GET YOU
# INTO MY LIFE

T he girls up front drank beer from plain, brown bottles. The more they drank, the mouthier Jeanie got. Alice stared out the window, tucking short strands of hair behind her ear as wind whipped around. She had no interest in navigating that particular minefield. Information was social currency Jeanie would exchange for power and status in her clique, and her gossip had played no small role in tarnishing Sue Chisholm's reputation, a friend of Denise's who was held back senior year because she'd gotten pregnant.

"Hey," Nalin called, leaning across and offering something to Alice.

When she looked over and saw the lit joint, her face screwed up. "No!"

Marylou and Jeanie turned back to see what Alice was complaining about.

"It's just grass," he insisted.

"I know." Her tone was imperious and told him she wasn't about to change her mind.

Jeanie grabbed the joint. "Don't be such a narc."

The blonde's statement was punctuated with a sneer from Nalin. Meanwhile, Kit continued to show Leo his magazine, more interested in the lives of people he never even met than everyone around him.

"That's Grace Jones," he explained.

Leo remarked, "She looks like she's made of plastic."

"She's *a*-mazing!" Kit had a way of talking about celebrities that made it seem like he knew them personally. Even Alice felt drawn to the conversation for a moment, but she couldn't find a way in. Kit continued, "And Andy Warhol lives with all his friends in this factory in New York."

"A factory?"

"Yeah," he said, then blurted out with a smile, "My mom knows him."

Laura had met Andy Warhol at a fabulous party in Toronto back when she was modelling. Whenever she told the story, Kit would listen to every detail as though hearing it for the first time. Often it felt that way, because with each telling of the tale, new particulars would surface. She was masterful at weaving the story, on occasion even putting on the very dress she had worn that evening.

It was a stunning gown, one that he never saw her in

outside of playing dress-up. There was never any cause for such extravagant formal wear in Antigonish. Dances and banquets at the local Legion hall certainly didn't call for it. She'd stand in his parents' bedroom in that shimmering designer dress, acting out her chance encounter with the artist. In their small suburban house in the middle of Nova Scotia, she looked so out of place. Like she belonged elsewhere.

Andy Warhol had invited her to New York that night. And the one thing that held her back from going was her own life. Kit never wanted to be in that position, to be disappointed because of his circumstances.

"No way!" Leo sat up, eyes wide. "Can I meet your mom?"

"Yeah." He gestured over to Alice. "Come with us."

Her jaw hung open for a second, then she called out to the driver, "Stop! Stop!"

"What—what is it?" Jack asked, panicked.

"Stop!"

All eyes were on her.

"Why?" Jack repeated, glancing around.

Her eyes shifted. "I forgot something important."

Kit finally turned to look at her, forehead creased with concern. "What?"

"My medicine," she said in a low voice as she tried to meet his already wandering eyes.

"What medicine?"

Alice raised her chin and explained with an air of importance, "The medicine I have to take for my allergies."

"What allergies?" Kit pressed.

"Well, we're not going back," Jeanie told them.

That was fine by Alice. "We'll hitch a ride back and then meet you at the beach later."

"What?" Kit said. "Why?"

Alice stared daggers through him and her words came through bared teeth. "My medicine. I could die."

Having no way to argue without calling her out on her lie, Kit resigned himself to the fact that they were on their own again. Jack pulled onto the side of the road and the two of them piled out of the car. It was a rural route, two lanes and not much of a shoulder to stand on. He got out to say a few parting words.

"So, you going to be okay?" His face showed genuine concern for her.

Alice slipped on both her satchel and a serious expression. "Yeah, yeah. I just have to take it every twelve hours. It's no big deal."

Standing off to the side with suitcase in hand, Kit watched the two of them. Jack had his hands on his waist, showing off broad shoulders and buff muscles. With Jack's head turned, Kit noted the cigarette tucked behind his ear. It was like it spawned there after every smoke.

"Okay," Jack said, stepping forward to stroke Alice on the arm. "We'll see you at the beach then."

"Yeah, for sure."

He gave a low wave. "See you later, Kit."

"I guess so," was all he could manage.

Gravel crunched as Jack returned to the car, slamming the door. Through the rear window, Leo gave Kit a smile, disappointment curled around the edges of it. As the Pontiac drove off, dust spun up and the boy waved a bittersweet goodbye. Kit stood in the middle of the road, staring off, completely oblivious to Marylou waving her hand from the passenger side window and Nalin scowling back at Alice. When the car crested a slight slope and disappeared from sight, he turned on Alice.

"What the hell?"

She shrugged her shoulders and put her palms out. "We're not driving with them."

"What? A ride all the way through to Sydney!" He pointed down the long stretch of asphalt.

"They're all drunk and stoned and everything. We could be killed," she reasoned, gesturing between them for emphasis.

His head tilted back slightly. "What are we going to do now?"

"Hitchhike," she said like it should be obvious. She peered away from him for signs of oncoming vehicles.

"Hitchhike," he repeated with a bitter laugh. "We had a ride all the way."

Alice folded her arms across her chest. "When are we having goodbye sex?"

"What?"

"When?"

"When we get there," he said, exasperated.

"It's not even goodbye sex," she noted, rolling her eyes. "It's hello sex since we never had sex, ever."

Kit didn't know how to respond; Alice didn't let him. She brought her hands together, twining her fingers anxiously.

"Maybe you don't even want to have sex."

The last time they had tried, he had pushed her away— actually physically pushed her. She almost cried. They were upstairs in his bedroom. His grandmother was at church and his dad was "out," which they both knew was code for scoring weed.

"What the hell?" she'd said.

"I—did you hear that? Somebody's home."

Then he'd risen from the bed and strode over to the window. Of course, nobody had been there. After he'd come back, both of them had lost the mood. Now his eyes shifted and he walked toward her, from the middle of the road, speaking gently.

"I do. Okay?"

"Do you?" Her voice was small.

"Yes," he declared. "I love you."

At those words, she softened, turning a questioning expression to him. "Do you really?"

"Yes."

Maybe that was enough, Alice thought, shuffling her feet, processing everything. Kit told her he loved her. And she loved him, even if she was still too hurt to admit it just now. She couldn't let him know she was jealous of the other kids in the car, so had acted rashly, throwing away their ride. The fact that he'd been more interested in Leo than in her was like a splinter she couldn't figure out how to remove from under her skin. It left her both annoyed and concerned. If she didn't deal with it, the wound would fester, but she couldn't bring the matter up now. Maybe she was overreacting. It wasn't the first time her temper had gotten her in trouble. The last thing she wanted was to ruin this day. The last day they'd spend together.

"Okay," she said.

With that, Alice turned and started walking along the side of the road again, continuing their journey toward Sydney. Kit walked by her side, glancing back for signs of traffic every so often. The asphalt was cracked in several places and the woods crowded in on either side of them.

"And anyway," she started, "I heard about these

girls—that they were hitchhiking—and they got in a car with a drunk driver, and they got stopped."

She paused on the road for dramatic effect. "The cop charged *everybody*." Her fingers splayed out in front of her to emphasize the last part.

"With what?" Kit asked.

"With drunk driving."

"Were the girls drinking?"

"No, but it doesn't matter."

"So they weren't drinking or driving."

"It doesn't matter," she insisted. "Okay? They got in the car. They knew the driver was drunk so they got charged."

"That seems a bit weird to me."

"Yeah, well, maybe," she began, then gestured with her index finger at him, "but that cop probably saved their lives."

Kit knew better than to argue any further. The best he could do was either go along with what she was saying or stay out of her way. What he admired most about Alice was the one thing that sometimes frustrated him beyond compare: once she got behind an idea, she would pursue it to the very end—her conviction was unrivalled. Sometimes, it meant getting carried so far away that she would reach an absurd point of no return, but even in the face of being utterly wrong, she wouldn't back down. He couldn't hold it against her when her passion was the very thing that made her who she was. Besides, love meant accepting someone for their true self. This was something Kit wished his father could accept, would accept.

"It's called having principles," she'd told him early on in their relationship.

"It's called being stubborn," he'd muttered back.

The entire foundation of their going steady was predicated on her single-minded intent to push them ahead. While Kit was perfectly happy with what they had, she kept trying to change things up. He loved Alice, it was true. But sometimes the things she wanted weren't the things that he wanted. Above all else, he was afraid that if she got her way, there'd be no going back to how things once were.

Their first kiss at the end of the school year had forced their friendship to evolve. What they had before then had been comfortable, easy. Now things were infinitely more complicated, and he was forever navigating her feelings, weighing them against his own. At the same time though, there was nothing he could have done to prevent things from changing.

When she had pressed her lips against his that time, he was taken aback. As the other students filled the hall, he didn't want to be the one to ruin everything. If he'd rejected her then, in front of everyone, she would have been humiliated and he would have given the guys in his class more ammunition against him. The name calling had subsided when he started hanging out with Alice. He was, if not cool, at least *not* lame by association. In that one moment with Alice, he fit into a teenage-shape cookie cutter mould, and he was okay with that, however briefly that kiss lasted.

It wasn't that he didn't want to be in a relationship. What he didn't want was what came with it—the expectation of something more, something he wasn't ready for. The level of commitment Alice expected from him was the very sort of thing that trapped people in towns like Antigonish. It almost happened to his own mother. As much as he couldn't afford to lose Alice, who understood him like no one else ever could, there was only so far he could walk down this path with her before they'd have to make a choice. In a perfect world, they'd both get what they wanted from each other. But this world was far from perfect.

After walking in silence for a bit, Alice slipped her hand into his. Their fingers twined together and she squeezed briefly. It was her way of saying she was sorry. He accepted the silent apology for now. Despite the vast stretch of nothing around them, they were stuck with each other. Even now, Kit had to admit to himself that there was nobody else he'd rather be stuck with.

# CHELSEA HOTEL

As they walked along the long stretch of road, Kit was desperate enough for a ride that he thumbed for the few cars travelling in their direction, disregarding Alice's earlier instructions. This time she didn't chide him for it, either. The beer run had cost them a significant amount of time. They hadn't even crossed the Canso Causeway to Cape Breton yet, and that was supposed to be the easy part of the trip.

When they'd talked about hitching their way to Sydney, Alice had made it sound simple, like she knew what she was doing, shrugging off Kit's initial concerns. She exuded a confidence that Kit wished he could pull off. Most days, he couldn't even convince himself to wear some of his favourite clothes for fear of calling more attention to himself.

After a few failed attempts at hitching a ride, Kit let out a frustrated sigh and stopped suddenly. Slowing her pace, Alice watched as he removed the *Interview* magazine from his luggage then sat on the upright case, flipping through pages. Following his lead, she took her camera out of her satchel and began framing shots. Neither one of them moved when the swoosh of a distant car was heard. On the surface, Kit was still annoyed with her for losing their ride—she'd have to make up for it by catching them another one. It was only after the oncoming vehicle drove by them that Alice turned around from looking through her camera lens.

"You just missed that one!" Kit complained, gesturing with the magazine in his hand. "You're too busy lining up the perfect shot. Pay attention."

She sighed but was otherwise nonchalant about the whole thing. "The light is good."

"They totally would have stopped for us."

"Let's go to New York instead," she suggested, rocking back and forth on her feet.

"Well, we'll have to go wait on the other side," he noted, "'cause New York's the other way."

Because it was all pretend anyway, Alice asked, "Why don't we though? I mean, you're running away from home, right? What's to stop us from making it all the way to New York?"

"I'm not running away," Kit corrected. "I'm going to live with my mom."

She fiddled with her camera, staring down at the lone digit on the counter that showed a single exposure left. Whatever picture she took next would be the final one on this trip. It would have to be a good one, a memorable one.

"I bet she'd be proud of you," Alice said. "If you made it all that way."

When Kit glanced over at her, she knew she'd caught his attention. A welcome reprieve from his moping, she wasn't about to let it go.

"We'd get an apartment," she continued. "In the East Village. To pay the rent we'd have to get work busing tables or washing dishes."

"But that'd be okay," he added agreeably, "because of the experience. You're supposed to suffer for your art, right? That's where all the good ideas come from. I'd write in my spare time and you could take pictures. One day you might even get a show at a local gallery."

Struck by an idea, Alice pointed at him. "You could write articles, too. Maybe get a piece published in *Interview*. And then you'd meet Andy Warhol. Just like your mom did."

As Kit gazed off, entranced by the fantasy playing out in his head, Alice made her way across the road. She was halfway to the other side before he noticed.

"Where are you going?" he asked.

She twirled around with arms spread wide and a broad smile planted on her face. "To New York! We'll live out a dream!"

It *was* a dream, Kit realized then. One day he'd make it a reality, but not today. Not with Alice. "We can't."

"Says who?"

"We don't have any money for a bus," he said. "And don't say we'll hitch. We can't even get a ride to Sydney. No, that's not right. We actually had a ride. We can't seem to keep one, though."

Another vehicle approached and this time Kit pointed to get her attention. Promptly Alice stuck her thumb out. Both of them watched as the car passed.

"If we'd stayed in the car, we'd probably be there now," he griped.

"It's not my fault," she defended, motioning to herself. "Nobody's stopping."

Kit scoffed. "Yeah, right."

"And nobody's stopping because of your stupid suitcase."

"I—I'm trying to hide it."

They glanced away from each other, tempers cooling slightly.

"What did you bring anyways?" she asked.

"Hardly anything." He clasped his magazine in both hands, holding it between his knees.

"Did you bring that shirt with the big sleeves?"

With raised eyebrows Kit said, "Yeah."

"What else?" she pressed, stashing her camera back in the satchel.

Getting up off his suitcase, Kit eagerly laid it down on its side. He knelt down with Alice, then clicked the clasps and opened it for her to rifle through the contents.

Pointing out a shirt, she noted, "This is new."

He made a face. "I . . . never wear it."

"Can I have it?" she asked with a playful smile.

"No!" he answered, like she had lost her mind.

She laughed. "Spaz."

While she scanned the road, he picked through his things and pulled something out. "Here, you can have this one."

Her eyes fell on his Edward Bear T-shirt, held out for her to view. It was one of his most cherished articles of clothing, worn with age, and had originated all the way from Toronto. Mr. Morash had gone to the city a few years ago to finalize his divorce on paper after a long period of being separated.

By that point, Kit had no illusion that his parents would work things out and that they'd return together. He knew because even his dad had stopped talking about the possibility. Gone were the days of "we'll see" and "maybe if." Instead, his dad returned with the shirt, which was more than Kit could have hoped for. The band had won a Juno award earlier that year, so when he wore the shirt to school the very next day, he seemed cool, for a brief period anyway.

Alice always felt he loved the shirt more for the fact that it came from the city where his mother lived rather than for the band itself. Because, as much as he enjoyed listening to their self-titled album on his dad's stereo, there were other musicians he loved more, like Elton John, or David Bowie. No, Edward Bear would somehow always be connected to his mom. For Kit to gift Alice with the shirt meant something.

"Really?" She took it from him, smiling sweetly.

If this was his way of making things right between them, he was doing a good job of it.

"Yes. You know, to remember me by."

Her smile faded. "I'm going to see you all the time though."

"Yeah, I know." He let out a nervous laugh while closing his suitcase.

Holding his prized possession in her hands, the reality of his leaving began to settle in. She only had a few hours left to convince him that moving to Sydney would be the biggest mistake of his life—of their lives. But how to go about telling him when he adored his mother so much?

She had overheard the whispered conversations about

Kit's mom at the kitchen parties that her own parents threw. At their annual shindig last Christmas, Alice had hidden under a table with the contraband lemon gin she'd swiped while her mother wasn't looking. As was customary, the women had gathered in the kitchen to gossip while the men wandered back into the living room. Although Alice had tuned their voices out for the most part, the clucking tongue of Beans's mom signalled some especially juicy bit of gossip. From under the tablecloth, Alice had to strain to hear them talking in low voices.

"What a sin, leaving that poor man on his own to look after a young boy," Beans's mom had commented. "Must be so hard this time of year, not having a whole family."

"A lesser man would've been too proud to move back in with his mother," another neighbour remarked.

"It's a wonder he hasn't met anyone after all these years. He's quite the catch."

"Oh, wouldn't *you* like to warm his bed!"

"I'll bet he's like a fine wine. Better with age."

"Joan, you never!"

"Shh! It wasn't like that! We were just kids back then. Besides, even if I didn't have my own man now, that woman broke Dave Morash."

They tsked collectively.

"Well, she was off her rocker anyway," Val cut in, always one to hold a grudge although Alice could never pinpoint why in this case. "She was a piss-poor wife and an even worse mother. Dave's better off without her. The lot of them are."

Beans's mom hushed them as someone came in from the living room.

"Ladies," Mr. Morash greeted them.

A couple of the women tittered.

"Are you empty?" Joan asked, not waiting for a response. "We've *got* to fix that for you. What're you having?"

"Rum and Coke."

"A man's got to quench his thirst, doesn't he?"

Alice rolled her eyes at Joan, who was laying it on thick.

He chuckled. "Right you are."

The sudden silence among them was broken by clinking ice, the hiss and pop of a Coke can opening, and various liquids being poured.

"I'll be out of your hair in a jiffy," he started in good humour, "so you can get back to talking about us fellas."

Awkward laughter followed.

"We were just reminiscing," Val assured him.

"The good old days, eh?" He patted his belly loud enough that Alice could discern the sound from where she was hidden. "Back when I was twenty pounds lighter."

"Oh, I'm sure you filled out just fine," Joan said.

"Cheers."

And with that, Alice assumed he left because the women burst out laughing shortly after.

"Joan, you're bad!" Beans's mom chided.

There were other times Alice had overheard adults talking, but the gist of it was always the same. Now she held this tangible thing that connected Kit to his mom, someone he put on a pedestal in spite of what everyone else thought about her. It was hard for Alice to admit that a part of her had been jealous of the woman she'd never met. Was that what drove the conversations at the parties? Jealousy?

With her eyes on Kit, she stood up, clasped the shirt between her legs and stripped off her top. Standing there with only her bra on, Alice watched him watch her. He kept his focus on the Edward Bear shirt he had gifted her, smiling in anticipation of her putting it on. She slipped it over her head, lips pursed.

"Yeah," he said in approval and she shrugged casually.

Happy to have the scent of him on her skin, she peered down the road again. As she stood by his side, she brushed back her hair with her fingertips, undoing the mess from changing.

"Everybody likes you, Alice," he told her, seated on his upright suitcase again.

Her eyebrows pressed together. "Nobody likes everybody."

For a while there was silence.

"But . . . everybody likes you," he repeated.

Her shoulder jerked. "I don't care."

Staring off wistfully, Kit said, "I wish everybody liked me."

She arched an eyebrow at him. Alice could say whatever was on her mind and people would always be okay with or at least deal with it. Whereas Kit was forever biting his tongue, too afraid to say the wrong thing, but always listening. People knew him as the son of the social studies teacher, Mr. More-Hash. The kid whose mother thought she was too good for their little town.

There were all these little details and stories built up around him, around his identity, that added up to one big falsehood about who he actually was. He couldn't act in any way outside of what was expected of him, the polite child of unfortunate circumstances. It felt like he was living a lie. That's part of why he had to leave. It wasn't because of Alice. He hoped she knew that.

"I wish you didn't care," she replied.

So did he. As he continued to stare into the distance, a familiar sound caught his attention. Both of them straightened their postures, thumbs out. A pickup truck slowed, then pulled up ahead of them.

"Yes!" Kit said, pumping his fist.

"Yes!" Alice agreed, laughing as she added, "Lucky!"

Both of them ran for the truck, Kit in the lead.

"I call the window!" she cried.

"No!"

When Kit opened the passenger-side door, he paused to let Alice get in. She stared up, all sense of humour departing from her like a flight of angels—the driver was an old and severe-looking priest. After clambering in after her, Kit shut the door. They drove on, hushed by the priest's presence, both vaguely worried they'd have their souls saved on this leg of the journey.

Alice had had bad luck hitching before, the one and only time she ignored the "No old guys alone" rule Denise had imparted to her the first time she set off, impetuously, to spend her babysitting money in the "big city" before starting high school. Not that she ever told anybody about it. Not even Kit. If she couldn't convince him to hitch back to Antigonish with her—and that was looking less likely as they got closer to their destination—she'd be on her own. For the first time in her life, that actually scared her.

# REBEL, REBEL

S olomon Books on Main Street was the first place Dave Morash thought to look, since his son always had his nose in a novel or periodical. En route, he worked through every possible reason he could fathom for Kit lying to him, going through a mental catalogue of all the things that had happened in the past week. To his mind, Kit wasn't acting any stranger than usual—he was excited about a new magazine that had come in; Alice had been over for Sunday dinner; earlier that day they'd had a fight about Lord only knew what, but Dave thought they'd resolved it.

When he entered the bookstore, a bell rang over the door, calling the owner's attention from behind the till. The older man was dressed in a suit despite the rising temperature, and his thinning hair was combed neatly to one side.

"O wind, rend open the heat / cut apart the heat / rend it to tatters," the shopkeeper recited, taking in a gust of air that swept through the premises.

"Afternoon, Bill," Dave greeted him with a polite smile.

"And a good day to you!"

Bill was quite a character, given to theatrics, and when Kit's mom had frequented the store, the two would delight in each other's company for the time it took her to pick out something for either Kit or herself. Mostly these days, Bill just quoted poetry at patrons, but back when Laura had been around, he'd oblige her with his knowledge of Shakespeare and recite parts. Dave could tell her mood by the characters Kit told him she had chosen on those days.

"Has Kit been by?" he asked in a casual manner, not wanting to let on that there was any sense of urgency.

"Indeed, just this very morning."

Dave perked up. "Did he say where he was going?"

"Alas, the lad didn't come in. I only saw his face, briefly pressed against the window to admire the newest display. Are you caught up in the sweeping family saga?"

It took him a moment to realize the bookseller was referring to the Kent family in the American Bicentennial Series. His eyes fell to the red, white, and blue balloons and banners up front that had so captivated his son just a few hours ago.

"No," Dave answered distantly. "Kit borrowed my copy."

"Well! You should have it back in no time. He's a

voracious reader and, as the critics are wont to say, that series is a real 'page turner'!"

Dave considered buying another book but feared getting dragged into a different conversation. Instead, he smiled and followed all the social cues necessary to extricate himself from the bookstore without hurting Bill's feelings. Dave Morash left Solomon Books no better off than when he had arrived at the shop. Outside, he rushed toward the Imperial Theatre, the second most likely place his son would be on a Saturday afternoon.

A group of kids was gathered outside, having just come out of a matinee of *Mother, Jugs & Speed*, the only movie advertised on the marquee. He strode toward them intending to ask after Kit without making it seem as though his son was in trouble.

"Have any of you guys seen Kit around?" he asked.

They shook their heads, eyes meeting in silent acknowledgement of how to respond. Mr. Morash was cool and everything, but he was also an authority figure and Kit, despite his townie ways, was still one of them. If he was up to something, they weren't about to say anything about it.

Glancing between the teens, Dave pressed further, "You sure you haven't seen him today?"

Still they shook their heads, some mumbling, "No." The town wasn't big enough to hide Kit anywhere else unless he was in the woods or over at someone else's house, and the latter was unlikely. With the exception of Alice, he didn't have many friends—none that Mr. Morash could name easily, anyway. The boy liked to read about far-off places and sometimes write stories about them, too. Most days, Kit had his head in the clouds, much like his mother, although Dave didn't care to think too hard about that—about her.

With no other options available, he drove back home. He raced along in his blue Datsun, holding a small spark of hope that there was some kind of misunderstanding and that Kit had returned home while Dave was out. That Joe had somehow mixed up the details of Kit and Alice's plans—it was, after all, the oldest trick in the book, each of them telling their parents they'd be at the other's house. If Dave wasn't so worried, he'd have laughed.

He'd pulled the same stunt with Kit's grandmother, many years ago, but in those days there wasn't anywhere to go, except to drive around and get up to harmless she-nanigans—underage drinking, fooling around with girls, general mischief.

His car peeled around the corner and into the gravel driveway, where he parked in front of the simple saltbox that he'd moved into with his mother. For a moment, he envisioned walking up the steps of the wooden front porch and entering to find Kit and Alice in the living room watching *American Bandstand* on TV. Even as he imagined it, he knew it was a nothing more than a flight of fancy.

Dave got out of the car and slammed the door shut behind him. With a huff he made his way toward the house, rubbing his temple. Out of the corner of his eye, he spied Beans riding by on the road out front.

He stopped in his tracks. "Beans!"

The kid kept riding but looked over at him. Beans had an older brother in Dave's social studies class just this past year, a freshman. They were cut from the same cloth, would talk a person's ear off if left to their own devices—the entire family was snoopy as all hell. Usually, Dave stayed tight lipped around them. As it was, there'd been enough chatter about the Morash family, and he certainly didn't need to fuel the fire. Today though, he suspected the boy's predilection toward knowing other people's business might be of use. Beans sure got around on that bicycle of his.

"Have you seen Kit?" Mr. Morash dug his fingers into his front pockets.

"Yeah." Beans rode his bike in circles.

"When?"

"Before."

"When before?"

"I don't know," he said. "Before."

Dave took a breath and glanced away, composing himself. "Where was he?"

"Over by Alice's."

Beans stopped at the top of the driveway.

"Was he alone?" Dave asked.

"No."

He spoke carefully, "*Who* was he *with*?"

"Alice."

He paused to think about what to say next in order to glean more helpful information from the kid. "Was this recently?"

"No," Beans said. "Before. Just after he left here."

Sensing the conversation would go no further, Mr. Morash backed away. "Okay. Thanks."

Turning toward the house, he was uncertain what he would do next. Let Joe and Val know? Know what? That Kit and Alice were out? It was still possible that was much was true.

Beans called out. "Is Kit really moving to Sydney?"

Dave froze. Slowly, he turned to look back at the kid, his eyes widening as though his whole world was falling down around him. And it very well could have been. Because Kit was gone. Not just gone, but heading into the eye of the storm.

# YOUNG HEARTS RUN FREE

The pickup truck rumbled along the broken asphalt. With a stern eye, the driver gave his two young passengers the once over. Kit glanced anxiously at the man's clerical collar, wondering if he could tell just by looking at them that they didn't go to church every Sunday.

"Is your name Christopher Robin, b'y?" the priest asked.

Kit shook his head, eyes darting over to Alice with concern.

The man jutted his chin toward her. "This one's Edward Bear. That's the proper name for Winnie-the-Pooh, eh?"

Smiling weakly, Kit explained, "It's the name of a band."

"That so?"

Alice nodded. "Yeah."

"What do they sing?"

Kit and Alice exchanged a look of restrained humour.

With a shrug, she sang a few refrains from "Last Song," and after a few lines the priest began to hum along, and when she stopped, to their surprise, he kept singing for a spell.

His voice trailed off. "Some good, that one."

"You know their music?" Kit asked, unable to contain his surprise.

"Lord works in mysterious ways," the man responded with a broad grin.

Suddenly, they burst out laughing, the song breaking the ice and opening the way for them to sing for a bit and make easy small talk easily. The priest drove them down coastline alongside rocky shores. Eventually, they crossed over a metal drawbridge signed *Welcome to Cape Breton*, after which it would only be a couple more hours drive to Sydney.

A diner at the side of the road was as far as the man could take them before he headed home. With smiles and waves goodbye, Kit and Alice stepped out of the pickup truck.

Sydelle's had bright decals on the front windows listing their main offering, *Family Size Fish & Chips*. It was a simple, square building with river-rock veneer on the front and white siding on the other walls. The diner's parking lot was riddled with potholes where water pooled.

Picnic tables were set up on one side of the lot, but

Alice and Kit were banking on air conditioning after the hot car ride. On their way in, Alice noted a pay phone and wondered if their parents or Kit's grandmother had figured out yet that they had lied about their whereabouts.

Inside, they ordered a plate of fries to share and a tall glass of milk each. They sat across from each other on hard, vinyl chairs. A long bar with vinyl stools affixed to the tiled floor lined one side of the diner. Specials were written on a blackboard behind the counter and the tables were covered with red and white checkered plastic, bottles of condiments lining the sides. Something about the setting made Alice think of Norman Rockwell's *The Runaway* painting, only she wasn't the one trying to get away. Maybe that made her the cop trying to talk sense into Kit, the wannabe hobo.

Thick black valances hung on the windows. A small fridge stood in the corner. Through the glass door, Alice could see cans of pop and round plastic vats on the top shelf. High up on a ledge in the opposite corner was a television tuned to American Bicentennial programming. She was constantly amazed at the fanfare from the United States; Dominion Day had just been celebrated on July 1 without nearly as much hullabaloo. She used to watch the *Festival Canada* program broadcast from Ottawa on television with her parents, but this year she couldn't deal with sitting down alone with her mother, without her sister or father.

Kit rolled up his sleeves to eat. They were the only patrons inside, and ate off the tray set between them. When they got down to the last of their fries, the waitress came by with another serving.

The woman was in her late forties, dressed in a mint-green uniform with a white apron and collar and a cap that held back only part of her feathered hair. A lit cigarette hung between her lips as she placed the paper plate on the table.

"We didn't order more fries." Alice pushed the plate back toward the waitress.

The waitress spoke around her smoke. "They're on the house."

"Thanks!" Kit exclaimed, thrilled. To Alice he added softly, "Lucky."

"So, where you two headed?" the woman asked as she cleared away their tray.

"Sydney," Alice answered with a smile.

With a coo the waitress teasingly asked, "So, you running away to get married?"

For a lark, Alice thought about saying yes.

"No!" Kit declared firmly, as though the waitress was completely off her rocker.

Alice stared at him, the corners of her mouth turning down a little. Not that she was one of those girls who dreamed of the perfect wedding, but his outright rejection of the idea hurt. Even before the acrimony between her parents, she could see the consequences of uttering the two simple words, "I do." Maybe Alice didn't want to marry Kit either—after all, it was a lifetime ahead of her—but with Kit's head so lost in the clouds, slipping away, he was clearly giving no thought to his comments to strangers and had a reckless disregard for her feelings. She pulled on the inside of her cheek to keep her feelings inside. She wasn't about to start a giant fight in the restaurant, not when they were so close to her goal and she'd already messed up so much by making them get out of Jack's car.

"I didn't think so," the waitress admitted, winking at Kit before she went back behind the counter.

He smirked. Alice watched him dig in to the fries. Still, although running away to get married was a fantasy, she didn't see why he couldn't just go along with it. The way he talked about Andy Warhol and friends, you'd think he lived in that factory with all of them. That was way more of a fairy tale than the two of them eloping. Alice stopped herself before saying *that* out loud.

Alice picked up a fry but tossed it back, suddenly losing her appetite, and, as another customer entered the diner, rushed Kit to finish, suddenly not wanting to hang around. They split the bill, then returned to the stretch of highway. The landscape here was distinctly rugged—to one side was the ocean; to the other, low brush with telephone poles extending as far as the eye could see. They walked in silence, but it wasn't long before Alice had to pee. In her need to escape the embarrassment of the diner, she'd forgotten to go before leaving. She moved off into the brush while Kit waited on the side of the road, running his fingers through his hair to lift it for the summer breeze.

"You don't have to live in Sydney, you know."

Andy Warhol appeared on his suitcase. He was dressed in a dark suit with a striped tie that was slightly askew. Kit glanced around to ensure nobody was nearby.

"You could just go for the summer," Andy Warhol added. "Your grandmother is a riot. Your father's cool."

With a scoff, Kit thrust his hands in his jeans pockets. "No, he's not."

"Why not?"

"My mother's cool," Kit amended with a smile, remembering the conversation he'd had with her over the phone earlier that week.

*Go confidently in the direction of your dreams!* his mother had said in her theatre voice, quoting a source he didn't know—that he almost never knew. There was so much he could learn from her. *Live the life you've always imagined.*

Would that it were so simple.

"She asked me to come and live with her," he added.

"Maybe she just meant for a visit."

He shook his head. "No, she didn't."

"It's a big deal, you know, moving." Andy Warhol stared into the sky, hands folded on his lap, listening to the sound of the ocean waves lapping on the shore. "I hate moving. Crabs have it the best."

"Crabs?"

"Crabs," he repeated, making a shape with one hand and scuttling it across imaginary sand. "Little crabs on the beach. They're always moving, but they always have their stuff."

Kit glanced away for a moment, blinking Andy Warhol away, then stared at his suitcase. He had packed hardly anything. It was a life lesson he'd learned on his very first day of kindergarten. His mom had been home on that occasion, and much ado had been made about his first day of school—new clothes, a *Batman* lunch box with matching steel thermos, and promises of joie de vivre!

That morning, his dad had had to speak gently through their bathroom door to tell her they were running late. When she finally appeared, he whistled. She, too, had done herself up, wearing a psychedelic dress of bright, swirling patterns with a hemline that graced her upper thigh. Kit thought she was the most beautiful thing he'd ever seen and that she'd done it all for him, in honour of his first day of school.

It was only after his dad dropped them off on his way to

work at the high school that Kit realized he'd left behind his favourite toy, Raggedy Andy. His mother had shooed him out of the bathroom where he'd placed it by the sink after his dad had warned them that they'd be late. In their rush to get out the door, Kit had forgotten about it.

Tears had welled in his eyes at the tragic oversight. All his new things for school couldn't make up for his old, beloved toy. His mom pulled him into her arms, coddling him. "Oh, sweetie. 'Happiness resides not in possessions' . . ." she whispered. ". . . 'happiness dwells in the soul.'"

With that, she had pressed a manicured finger to his heart. It might as well have been an arrow piercing his chest. His five-year-old self didn't understand—couldn't comprehend—any sort of existence without Raggedy Andy. Like the slow windup of a siren, he began to wail, and once he started, he was utterly inconsolable.

His mother had been desperate to contain the outburst, glancing around at the other mothers who were in control of their children. Mascara ran around her damp eyes. Kit wound up ruining the first day of school for the both of them. It was only years later that he remembered what she'd told him, and the words began to carry real meaning.

She always had wise sayings she could pull from thin air, by virtue of being so well read and worldly, and having so many interesting life experiences. Often, she'd meditate and practice yoga, reading philosophical books like *Zen and the Art of Motorcycle Maintenance.* That was exactly what he needed in his life right now, to live a lighter existence. When he'd packed that morning, he remembered what his mother had said that one time in kindergarten, that the weight of possessions could drag a person down both literally and figuratively.

Alice called out, "I'm not carrying your suitcase."

She came up from the shallow ditch doing up her pants, meaning what she said. Kit gave her a look that said he'd never expected she would carry his suitcase, but it wasn't worth another fight. Without responding, he picked up his luggage and continued walking with her across the rugged coastline to the Cape Breton Highlands. No cars passed for a long while.

They wound their way up a steep incline, following the guardrail. The highway curved along the side of lush, green mountains. Several roadside look-offs had been built so tourists could safely pull over and take in the panoramas and wildlife. But the truth was, after walking for an hour in the heat, it all started to look the same. The sight of his scuffed shoes and the ache in his feet just reminded him that all this rustic wilderness was what he wanted to get away from—he longed for skyscrapers, crowds of people, swathes of traffic, voices overlapping, and car horns honking.

On their family trips to Halifax once or twice a year,

Kit would revel in the bustling cityscape along Barrington Street and Spring Garden Road. He'd head to the Woolco store at the Scotia Square shopping centre with his grandmother while his dad would hit up Sam the Record Man. All the while, Kit would people watch, taking in fashion, mannerisms, turns of phrase.

At lunch they'd eat at the Lord Nelson Hotel, where Kit admired the artists and former hippies, who radiated coolness. The place recently garnered more of Kit's interest owing to a novel called *Lord Nelson Tavern*, inspired by the hotel. His dad had picked up a copy on a pre-Christmas trip last year, and Kit had torn through it on their ride back to Antigonish. It was about a group of university students who hung out at the tavern to gossip and philosophize, all while pining after a vain and unattainable girl. What's more, the author was from small-town Nova Scotia. It gave him hope for his own writing career.

A rustling from the steep cliff below, on the other side of the guardrail, made Kit realize they weren't alone. He wasn't sure which would be worse, a moose or a black bear. The sad thing was, that would be the most exciting thing to happen in his life—death or mauling by wild animal. He shuddered at the thought. Alice didn't seem bothered in the least. Instead, she simply took it all in, enchanted by the scenery and looking like she wished she had another roll of film.

"Once upon a time . . ." she started, dreamily.

"What?"

"Make a story."

". . . they walked along the road," he said.

She waited for him to finish, but he didn't. ". . . they walked along the road and . . ."

Even though Kit enjoyed writing, even considered himself a writer and wanted to pursue it as a career some day, he wasn't very good at coming up with stories on the spot. It took time to develop something clever. Sometimes, several balls of crumpled paper would pile up in his waste bin before he wrote anything good enough to share.

Being put on the spot made him uncomfortable. Besides, he was already tired. Too tired to put creative energy into anything. Alice didn't understand that writing wasn't like taking a picture. He couldn't just press a button.

". . . they walked along the road," he repeated, dully. "Walking and walking. The boy wore shoes and the girl wore runners. It was the longest day at the end of the world."

Their feet crunched along the gravel shoulder, the long day's journey pressing down on them.

"She didn't want him to go, but he was going to go anyways," Kit continued. "It was the end of the world."

She frowned. "That's a depressing story."

Some time ago they'd had a conversation about fiction—

a bit of a debate, actually. Where he felt stories could end in any manner depending on the writer's intent, Alice firmly believed that fiction of any kind was meant purely for escapism, and that stories had to end happily. He dismissed her opinion outright. It was a writer's prerogative to end a work any which way he wanted.

Of course, she fought him on it; she always did. So he relented and called it the Lesley Gore method of writing, sometimes humming "Sunshine, Lollipops and Rainbows" at the end of a movie that met Alice's criteria for good fiction.

Now, he drew deep from his energy for more verve and added the happily ever after he knew she was looking for. "And then a helicopter flew in that picked them up and took them to New York where they lived with Andy Warhol. And the guy with shoes, well, he wrote books. The girl in the runners, she took pictures."

"And the boy's mom came to live with them in New York," she added with levity.

He chuckled. "And the world ended everywhere, but not in New York."

"And there was a party."

"Every night was a party," he threw in.

"Forever," she declared.

But even Alice wasn't sure if she believed the fiction this time.

# GUYSBOROUGH TRAIN

**D**ave stood by the living-room window, distraught. One hand was propped up against the wall, the other on his hip, as he stared out from behind the translucent curtain, hoping to catch movement in the yard.

It was quiet inside now. No television, no stereo. Just the silence of a house that was missing someone. A white poinsettia thrived by the window beneath two framed prints, one of a boy and the other of a girl, both in Regency-era clothes. On the opposite side of the window was an art quilt. Kitty-corner to that was a pair of botanical studies. The room was a mishmash of things brought together after Dave and Kit's lives had been upturned.

Now Kit was headed right into the eye of the storm that had caused all this turmoil to begin with. It was because of *her* that Dave had to move back in with his mother. It wasn't that he believed a single man couldn't raise a son on his own, without a woman's influence. Truth be told, he felt he'd done a decent job of bringing Kit up without much help.

But what the boy needed during his formative years was to know what normalcy looked like. And Dave's mom sure provided that—things had to be done a certain way in her house, and as much as Dave, a grown man, was loathe to abide by some of her house rules, he did it for the good of his son. Now he hovered over his vinyl collection, no comfort to him now, as his mother stood nearby.

"Why would he take Alice with him?" he asked.

"At least he's not alone," she offered, scratching her temple as she moved toward the sofa.

He put his hands in his pockets, not sure what else to do with them. A sense of helplessness overcame him; standing around waiting felt counterproductive.

"Should I call Val and Joe?"

"No." She plunked herself down and waved him off. "They'll just worry."

His forehead creased. "You're not worried?"

Mrs. Morash looked up at the ceiling and swayed her head from side to side. "Well, he's fifteen. You took a lot of trips when you were fifteen."

Crossing her legs, she wagged a finger at him to emphasize her point. A swath of memories cut through him—the things he got up to when he was Kit's age couldn't be repeated to his mother. If she'd known what he'd been up to all those times he'd gone away, she wouldn't be so cavalier about Kit missing now. How one of his buddies would take his dad's car for a joyride and they'd cruise around smashing rural mailboxes with baseball bats. Or that one time he'd pinched some of his father's whisky and gone out to the woods to drink and get to third base with Joan Pettipas.

The closest he ever came to real danger was crossing the train trestle on dares, like that one time his shoe got caught in the tracks when a train was coming. As he twisted, trying to free his foot, one of other the boys alerted him to the oncoming train. It was a joke, so he thought until a whistle pierced the air, driving him to panic as he tried to free himself.

In his mind, he imagined losing his foot, just like every adult ever warned, and the more he struggled to free himself, the more stuck his shoe felt. Then, one of his friends leaped out of the tall grass, loudly blowing a wooden train whistle. He punched the prankster hard in the arm and the boys had a good laugh at his expense. He was always a bit more cautious after that. A real train conductor wouldn't have seen him beyond the tall grass.

"I have to go and get him," he said now with urgency as he strode across living room, gesturing toward the front door.

"Okay, but if you do that, then you stopped him." She shook her head. The singsong quality in her voice drove Dave nuts.

He paused for a moment to consider what she was saying before coming back to the living room. "And I'm not supposed to stop him?"

She huffed. "She'll call."

"Alice?"

He paced back to the window. It seemed unlikely. Of the two of them, Kit was the more responsible—with the astounding exception of running away from home.

"No, Laura will call," she reasoned.

At the mention of his ex-wife's name he turned. His mother had only ever seen the tip of the iceberg. The version she knew of the very first time he met Kit's mother had been altered to resemble the sort of fairy tale Laura often liked to spin as her stories. They'd met in Halifax as students. He was getting a teaching degree at Saint Mary's; she was studying theatre at Dalhousie.

One night at a mixer, she appeared next to him. He was high at the time, smoking a joint on the back deck of a frat house. Despite the poor lighting of a bare bulb overhead, she had an ethereal glow. He was slow to open his mouth, and before he could get a word out, one of the pledges swung the screen door open, chasing after her. The frat boy grabbed her arm but she pulled away brusquely. Dave watched, amused as she spun on her heel and unleashed a verbal diatribe on the unwitting recipient.

To which the boy responded, "Don't be like that."

When he reached for her again, she stepped away, nearly toppling Dave over. Her surprised expression made it clear she hadn't seen him until then.

"Are you just going to stand there?" she demanded. "Can't you recognize a damsel in distress when you see one?"

"What's more to say?" He gestured to the pledge with the joint still in his hand. "You told that fella he's stunned. Unless . . . maybe he's too stunned to understand?"

Two things happened in the next instant: Laura swiped his joint, and the frat boy punched Dave. A fight ensued, though it didn't last very long. Shortly after, a rowdy crowd poured into the backyard and one of the neighbours yelled something about calling the cops. Some guys pulled the two of them apart, breaking up the minor brawl.

Dave staggered off down the street, slightly worse for wear, having taken a couple of punches to his face and torso, and when a thin arm wrapped around his waist, he was startled to see Laura smiling up at him.

"It turns out you're my white knight after all."

"You didn't look the type that needed saving."

"Oh, sweetie." She stopped them in their tracks,

placed a palm on his cheek and gazed deeply into his eyes. "Everyone needs to be saved."

He swallowed hard. "What do you reckon I need saving from?"

After taking a deep inhale of the joint she'd stolen off him, she got up on her tiptoes and kissed him. Smoke filled his mouth. She pulled away with a smile, then burst out laughing, not giving a response. Years later, there'd be no humour in the answer he'd discover. Not everything in life had an air whistle to warn of danger ahead of time.

As calmly as he could manage now, Dave told his mother, "She will *not* call."

"Okay." She put a hand up in half surrender. "Kit will call."

He spread his arms out in exasperation. "So, I'm just supposed to wait for him to call?"

Mrs. Morash sat forward, her expression soft and voice ever-so gentle. "Let him find out for himself."

For a long while they just stared at each other. Kit lived so much in his own head that the memories of his mother were probably mixed up with some fictionalized version of the woman. Dave knew better—knew her intimately better—for both good and bad. There had been a long time when he had tried to bury the bad, too. It would be better for Kit to peel the bandage off quickly.

With that idea settled within him, he nodded in agreement. It was time Kit knew. He was old enough now. Wasn't he?

# CARRY ME

Too tired to continue walking, Kit and Alice hunkered down at a bend in the road at the top of a hill where the land plateaued—it had gotten to that point where no matter how much they wanted to get to Sydney, they were too tired to continue walking.

At that point, they also had nothing to left to say to each other. A gentle breeze kissed their skin as the sun descended in the sky. They heard the next car before they could see it, and when the vehicle rounded the curve, they both leaned forward, trying to assess the likelihood of success before making the effort to get up. Even from a distance, the light mounted atop the roof of the RCMP cruiser was visible.

"Oh damn, oh damn!" Kit muttered. "Unlucky."

"No, no," Alice argued, moving to stand. "That's lucky."

As they got up, Alice patted her hands together to displace dirt and gravel before sticking out a thumb.

"Hitchhiking's illegal," he told her.

For a fragment of a second she glanced back at him. "N-no, it's not."

"It isn't?" He was completely perplexed as the cruiser pulled over.

They fumbled with their baggage for a moment, neither completely convinced of who was right. Remembering suddenly that she had brought contraband, Alice reached into her satchel.

"Lemon gin!" she blurted.

He panicked. "Dump it!"

On the sly, she tossed the bottle into the bushes at the side of the road. They ran ahead and got into the back of the cruiser. Without a word, the officer pulled onto the road and accelerated. Trees swooshed by as they travelled along the highway, making up for lost time. It was dead quiet in the car except for the faint buzzing of the wireless radio and the occasional voices on the other end.

From the back seat Alice stared, enthralled by the dials and the fact that she was in an actual RCMP cruiser— *without* having committed a crime.

By her side, Kit shifted uncomfortably and mouthed, "Are you sure?"

She considered, not actually a hundred per cent certain.

There was only one way to find out for sure, so she went straight to the source, asking the officer, "Is hitchhiking illegal?"

The officer took a long, hard look at them in the rear-view mirror. "Are you two lawbreakers?"

"No," Kit replied, adamant.

"Well," he stated, "there you go then."

Neither of them could tell if he was smiling because of his thick mustache. It was just like the one on Constable John Constable on *The Beachcombers*, only this guy didn't look nearly as friendly. Kit and Alice exchanged a concerned look because it didn't seem like he'd given them an answer.

"Where are you headed exactly?" the officer asked.

"Sydney," Kit answered.

"Dominion Beach," Alice corrected with a knowing smile.

That caught the cop's attention. "What's going on at Dominion Beach tonight?"

"Nothing," Kit lied.

Recognizing her misstep, Alice shifted her gaze. "Just Sydney is where we're going."

Penitent, she looked over at Kit, who had distress written all over his face: lips pursed in a fine line, eyebrows pinched in the middle. He needed to relax if they wanted to get all the way to Sydney in time for the party. If the officer sensed Kit was anxious about something, Alice was sure they'd be busted.

The dispatcher's voice came through the radio. "Fifty-five, if you're in the area we have a code one minor MVI just off the 105."

The officer picked up the handheld and spoke into it. "En route. Over."

For the first time in her life, Alice wondered what a code one minor MVI was and if they'd be involved in some kind of high-speed chase or shootout, like in the movies.

Perhaps reading into their expressions, the office said, "Just a little mishap. Nothing serious."

Kit whispered anxiously, "Lucky or unlucky?"

"I don't know," Alice replied in a hushed voice.

They arrived on scene to find a car that had smashed into the side of a red barn. *Motor Vehicle Incident—MVI*, Alice figured. By the left rear wheel of the Pontiac Bonneville, a folding table was knocked over, and a pitcher and glasses were flung across the lawn. Smoke billowed from the hood of the vehicle. On the driver's side, two men were in a heated dispute.

One man had long hair and a scraggly beard. He wore a baggy shirt and equally loose pants. The other man was much older, frail looking, hardly able to stand on his own two feet. He had on a fisherman's cap and lightweight jacket. His dazed eyes stared from behind wire-rim glasses.

"Vernon, there's no two ways about it," the bearded man said. "You's sauced."

"Go 'way, b'y! Whaddya know?"

"I knows that you gets to the Hall every Saturday for a scoff and some drinks, and sure as there's piss in a cat you comes bounding down that road drunk like a fish. Other times you've busted up McGilvery's mailbox, knocked over Boisseau's fence, and you once ripped apart the widow Sparling's planters. And now you've gone straight through me barn!"

"Ah, you're being a sook. I barely touched the barn. Paint's not even chipped."

The officer got out of the cruiser, putting on his hat as he walked over to the two men.

"What's this now, you called the law?" the older man asked as he straightened his fisherman's cap.

"You're not fit to be on the road."

"By Jesus, you're gonna drive me to drink!"

"Vernon, you gone drove yourself already, you old coot."

As the officer approached, the two men moved around the car to greet him. The older one staggered up a slight incline, then teetered and fell back onto the trunk of the car. He remained there, propped up by the vehicle that was still smoking on the other side.

"If you want to see someone who's drunk, *he's* drunk," Kit observed.

"Yeah, no kidding."

"Who's that other guy?"

The bearded man gestured at the drunk while talking to the officer and bringing him around the vehicle to inspect the damage. It didn't look like the car had been travelling very quickly, Alice surmised. There were no skid marks and the barn wall was still fairly intact.

Meanwhile, the drunk tiptoed over to take a swig of something from one of the glasses on the ground. It was almost comical the way he was standing, one hand out to keep his balance as he leaned down low.

"He probably lives in that brown house," Alice finally answered.

She watched the RCMP officer carefully, fascinated by the whole crime scene investigation. He'd taken a notepad off his utility belt, which also held a billy club and hand-cuffs, and was now scribbling down his observations. Craning her neck to get a better view, she wondered if he had a gun, too.

"What brown house?" Kit asked, putting his elbow up on back of seat and twisting around to get a better view of their surroundings.

Her eyes went bright. If she were a cartoon, a light bulb would have been glowing above her head. "You know what?"

"What house?" he repeated.

"I think I want to be a cop," she declared. Nothing had been clearer to her in her entire life.

He didn't seem to be listening. "What house, Alice?"

"It's—you can see the corner of it." Turning around in her seat she pointed.

"I can't see anything."

Both of them stared out the rear window. He continued to scan the area while she couldn't believe he was interrupting her epiphany with something so trivial as a stupid brown house—which was also clearly in plain sight.

"Really?" she asked. "It's right there. It's, like, right behind that one."

The cruiser door slammed shut and the ignition started, siren blaring. Another more pressing incident must have come up. Kit and Alice turned to face forward in their seats. To their alarm, the old drunk was behind the steering wheel.

The very sight of him caused them both to scream, setting off a chain of reactionary events. Startled, the man glanced back at them, equally surprised, and he let out a terrified cry of his own.

"Holy Jesus!" he slurred, breath thick with booze. "Holy mother of God!"

But instead of getting out of the car, he hit the gas. The cruiser veered unsteadily as the drunk floored it, Kit and Alice continuing to screech in the back seat. The cruiser sped up, churning up dirt as it spun out of control. Beyond any reasonable doubt, Alice was certain that they were all going to die in an MVI. But the drunk didn't get far—through some sort of inebriated muscle memory, he drove the cruiser toward the barn just on the other side of the first car he had crashed. Thankfully, he slammed on the brakes before impact.

The driver was hauled out by the officer, who paused to unlock the back door so Kit and Alice could stumble out of the car in a daze. Backup was called to the scene while the two of them stood and stared at the near miss. When the other officer arrived, he and the bearded man took charge of the drunk. The old man had given himself a fright, and was visibly shaken by the unexpected company he'd encountered in the cruiser.

The first officer came back to his cruiser, walking tentatively toward Kit and Alice. "Everybody's okay, right?"

"Yeah," Kit murmured, rubbing the back of his head.

Heart racing with adrenaline, Alice gazed in awe at what had just happened. She'd never felt so alive.

"Because I probably shouldn't have had you in the car," the officer admitted, gingerly coming around to them, like they were wild animals. "But everybody's okay, so we don't need to mention anything about this."

Alice folded her arms across her chest, head tilted as she clued in to what he was saying.

"No way," Kit agreed, glancing over at her, hands in pockets. "Yeah, everything's okay."

The officer scanned their faces, nodding while he spoke, as if to subliminally coerce them to agree. "So, the cruiser's okay. You're okay. Everything's okay. So let's get you to Sydney."

Knowing an opportunity when it presented itself, Alice casually suggested with a knowing smile, "If you could take us straight to Dominion Beach, that would be extra okay."

"You got a deal," he said.

Her smile broadened into a grin and they all got back into the cruiser. Driving along a rocky shoreline, the sunset glimmered on the water's surface. Alice beamed, relishing the warm rays on her face and their good fortune of getting a ride all the way to the party. Kit had worry painted on his face, even as they got closer to their destination.

"Want me to turn on the siren?" the officer asked.

"No!" Kit shook his head, brow furrowed.

"Yes!" Alice urged, face bright with delight.

She loved everything about this moment—her decision to be a police officer and that life would be *this* exciting all the time.

While the siren wailed, she quietly said to Kit, "Lucky."

Just after dusk, light flashing on rooftop, the cruiser blared into Sydney, announcing their arrival. Industrial buildings crowded the outskirts, but as they got deeper into the city, they saw more and more storefronts, one with a big sign that read *Pools & Hot Tubs*.

Kit and Alice gazed, bright eyed, out the window at the lights of the big city. Sydney boasted a population of thirty thousand. It was huge compared to their small town, and Saturday night on the main drag here was more lively than anything they'd ever seen back home. On the sidewalks, crowds of people were dressed for a night out, some heading into bars and restaurants. The marquee on the theatre displayed showtimes for premiere movies like *All the President's Men*. There were even a few sketchy characters hanging around street corners, alert to the RCMP cruiser's flashing presence.

Alice was no stranger to the streets of Sydney. Her mom's sister, Jackie, had settled here and up until recently, Alice's family would drive up to visit every summer. Now with her parents separated, Denise in Halifax, and her cousin Linda in Moncton, it had been a while since their last trip.

Her cousin Terry was supposed to be at the party but had been grounded a few days ago. All four of the girls had gone to Dominion Beach together last summer; it was where all the teens hung out to drink around bonfires. But as much as she was nostalgic for all the times she'd hung out with her sister, Denise, and their cousins, Alice was excited about the promise of making new memories here with Kit.

To him, it was all new. The bright lights and bustling streetscape were a welcome sight. It wasn't New York City—hell, it wasn't even Halifax. There was too much green space and too few skyscrapers to be the kind of city Kit dreamed of living in. But this was home. At least for now. The officer drove straight through to the other side of downtown Sydney before pulling off by the parking lot near the boardwalk, where a few people were out for evening strolls. They got out of the cruiser, and Kit set his suitcase down by the driver's side as he stood next to Alice.

Rolling down his window to talk to them, the officer pressed his arm across the window frame, one hand on the steering wheel as he leaned out slightly. "So the beach is just over the road and down the path through the brush."

As the man spoke, Kit stared into the darkness, trying to get a visual. There were a few street lights in the lot behind them, but otherwise he could only make out tall grass. It was Alice who had heard of the party and had wanted to go.

"Great, yeah, we know," Alice said. "Thanks."

"There's no wild party going on tonight is there?"

"No," Kit answered.

Not trusting herself to talk after almost giving them

away before, Alice shook her head, hair flapping around her face.

"A party is no problem," the officer started to assure them, "but a wild party . . . that would be not so good. Got it?"

"Yeah, no wild party for sure," she told him, convinced that it wasn't even a lie. One person's idea of wild was another's version of lame. "You got a deal."

"You take care."

"Thanks," Kit said. "Bye."

The officer's hand came down to pat the cruiser door and he drove off. No sooner had the vehicle pulled away than Kit pumped his fist.

"Lucky!"

"Lucky twice!" Alice agreed, holding up two fingers.

Turning toward the path, he brushed the back of his hand against her arm. "Come on."

They headed down the road toward the beach, taking the boardwalk before cutting through brush as instructed. Kit lost his footing a few times, his platform shoes wobbling in the uneven surface beneath him. It was bad enough they were so scuffed from the long day of walking, and now sand crept in. Even still, he wasn't about to take them off. This was a party after all; his shoes were his best foot forward, literally.

Off in the distance, a few campfires glowed brightly. It

was much cooler by the water, especially now that the sun had fully set. Alice pulled a hooded knit cardigan from her satchel.

"My shoes are getting wrecked," Kit lamented.

"I told you." She looked him up and down before stepping away, leaving him to rue his fashion choice and the state of his favourite shoes.

"I told you," Andy Warhol repeated her words, hugging his elbows in the chilly air.

Kit frowned. He didn't want a know-it-all for a spirit animal. Instead, he embraced the ways of the hermit crab, scuttling off to the beach with his small suitcase.

Andy Warhol hung back and announced, "There they are."

The party was in full swing with about twenty teenagers crowded around, some sitting on folding chairs, but most huddled by the fires. One girl ran around with two sparklers held over her head, laughing. Kit trudged across the sand, navigating over a driftwood log toward the party.

Music blared and as he neared, the figures came more into focus, dancing around the fires. Most of them had jackets or sweaters on over their summer clothes. Alice had disappeared to find her friends. This whole night was about her—the beach party and the promise of sex.

It was normal at his age for a boy to have a girlfriend,

or at least to want to have one. While it was true that he loved Alice, who understood him in a way that no one else did, he couldn't tell her he didn't want everything that came with being in a relationship. No, that wasn't quite right. Kit couldn't tell her what he wanted from a relationship. And if he couldn't admit it to Alice, who knew him better than anyone, Kit didn't know if he'd ever be able to admit it to anyone. Maybe she'd never forgive him. And as for his dad, he already knew where the man stood. It was this combination of certainty and uncertainty that had given Kit his reasons for leaving.

He didn't really know anyone at the party except for Leo. And aside from that one exception, Kit wasn't particularly interested in being there. He only agreed to go to Dominion Beach for Alice's sake. If his mother knew about Alice, she would say their relationship was yin-yang—they were contrary but complementary. That's exactly how Kit felt about his girlfriend. He did things for her that went against his nature because her happiness was inexplicably tied to his own.

And so, being at the party was a small price to pay. Alice had helped him get to Sydney, after all. He'd make the best of the night before seeing his mom in the morning. From the crowd, Jeanie came forward and wrapped her arms around Kit. She had a beer in one hand and reeked distinctly of pot.

He froze in her embrace. Jeanie wasn't exactly nice. In fact, Kit figured he was among the last people she'd want to be seen with, but under the influence of drugs and alcohol she was warm and friendly. Everyone put on some kind of a façade, though, and maybe hers was the clichéd mean girl.

Away from the usual social circles in their small town, Jeanie didn't have to pretend. Or maybe she just knew he was moving away and she'd never have to deal with him again. Regardless, when Jeanie pulled back, she handed him her beer, which he drank from both to quench his thirst and to push down the anxiety he felt from not having the comfort of her younger brother around. Talking to Leo had put him at ease in the car, but now he feared he'd have to hang with a bunch of people he hardly knew for the rest of the night.

Jeanie led him to the rest of the group on the other side of the fire, where he was welcomed by Jack and his friends like a long, lost friend. Alice was already in the thick of things. Drinking and laughing, she was getting pulled in to the clique. In a way he was relieved. It meant she might get too drunk for them to fool around, and he could just enjoy the party without the added pressure. He wanted their last night together to be memorable, not uncomfortable, and he wanted a way out.

While Alice stood amid the others, Kit found himself

on the outside of the circle, alone and in search of the only other person he knew on the beach. If he was really lucky, he'd find what he was looking for.

# NO TIME

**K**it hadn't actually thought to bring a jacket. When his grandmother mentioned it earlier that day, he didn't want to tip her off about his suitcase. Now he regretted the oversight, setting his luggage down by a cooler so he could roll his shirt sleeves back down and button the cuffs.

Sitting on driftwood with some of the others, Nalin puffed on a joint. Even he didn't have quite the same edge as he did in the car. The sneer was mostly gone from his demeanour, replaced by sarcastic joking.

Trying to make the most of the evening, Kit swayed to the music. Self-conscious, he mimicked what he saw around him, keeping his arms low and close to his body, feet planted firmly in the sand, moving his hips. When the joint made its way around to him, he took a drag.

Dancing around in one spot, he also took a swig from a bottle that was handed to him, and it burned. Promptly wiping a hand over his face, he turned the bottle over in his hand to see it was some brand of rye whisky. His head swam. With a surreptitious glance around, he found a girl to hand it off to, then stepped away.

Alice took note of him distancing himself from the crowd as Jack and his friends talked. The sleeves on her sweater were too long but they kept her fingertips warm as she brushed the hair from her eyes. Jack stood next to her, smiling and laughing. As much as she wanted to enjoy his company and be a part of the conversation, she couldn't help but notice Kit's aloofness.

Even though he was just a couple metres away, Kit might as well have been an ocean away the way he looked off into the distance like he was searching for something more. Like she wasn't enough. But then, she was never enough for him. Nearby, Nalin stood behind Marylou, one hand clasped across her shoulder, the other holding the whisky bottle that was making its rounds. He was talking to Jack as though Alice wasn't standing right by his side. In a way she wasn't, too preoccupied watching Kit to give Jack her full attention.

"Denise is a year ahead of you," Nalin observed. "Alice is a year behind you." Then he reached out and shook her by the shoulder to transport her back to the conversation. "Maybe you have a better chance with Alice."

Jack laughed, looking down coyly. "Shut up."

A moment later, Kit's eyes landed on Leo, who sat amid a circle of empty chairs except for one with a guitar placed upright in it. He had a pullover surfer sweater on, and leaned into the fire from his seat. Alone, like Kit felt.

Meanwhile, Nalin kept playing matchmaker, saying to Alice, "Jeanie's not his girlfriend."

"Yeah, she knows that," Jack said.

"Does Jeanie?" Marylou asked.

Jack looked away, in an attempt to be cool about it. Alice didn't notice. She was focused on Kit wandering off. Pulling the front of her cardigan closed, she crossed her arms to keep herself warm. Was he upset about the others talking as though they weren't a couple?

"Jack wants Denise," Nalin tattled.

"Shut up, Nalin," Marylou chided.

Not to be silenced, he added, "You know, you're prettier than Denise."

Alice shook her head. "No, I'm not."

"Shut up, Nalin!" Marylou repeated, turning to place her index finger over his lips.

He stepped back, but she pursued him and they started making out.

"Yes, you are," Jack said with a nonchalant shrug.

Throwing him a furtive smile, Alice began swinging her arms at her sides. They couldn't look at each other. Her stomach flipped over a couple of times, sensing that he wanted her in ways that Kit never did. And in that brief moment, with the alcohol swimming in her head, she didn't feel guilty about wanting him back.

In the distance, Leo leaned forward with his hands clasped near the fire. He was intent on the flame and the warmth it provided. When he caught sight of Kit, he immediately brightened and got up.

"Hey, how's it going?" Leo's arms lifted as though he was going to hug him, but Kit held out a hand and they shook instead.

"It's good," Kit said.

Leo gestured to the cooler. "Do you want a beer?"

"Yeah, thank you."

Taking a bottle out, Leo fumbled with an opener and let the cap drop on the sand before passing the beer to him. "There it is."

"Cheers."

"Yeah, definitely."

As they sat down, swigging from their drinks, Leo pulled his seat closer. For a while, they continued making awkward small talk, but as the night grew long and as Leo drank more, the conversation became easier. Soon they were back to how things had been in the car, a sense of ease and lightheartedness coming over them.

"So, do you like music?" Leo asked, then he laughed at himself, running a hand through his mess of hair, which

Kit began to recognize as a nervous tic. "Everyone likes music. I mean, who do you listen to?'"

"I listen to a lot of stuff . . . Queen, the Bee Gees, David Bowie. If I had to pick a favourite though, it'd definitely be Elton John."

"He wears the craziest costumes!"

"That's exactly why I'd love to see him in concert," Kit said. "Can you imagine him dressed up like the Statue of Liberty, or Donald Duck?"

"Is it true he wore glasses that spelled his name in lights?"

"Yes! They cost five thousand dollars."

"No way! That's weird."

Not wanting to admit that was part of the musician's appeal, Kit pushed the conversation in another direction. "My dad has a huge vinyl collection. We listen to a lot of different music."

"Your dad's super cool."

Kit shrugged.

"That must explain why you are, too," Leo added.

Their eyes met and they smiled awkwardly at each other.

"He has a big-ass stereo," Kit continued, breaking off his gaze. "It's, like, state of the art. You should come over some time and listen."

"Yeah?" Leo lit up.

Kit nodded. "For sure."

Alice watched Kit and Leo for a spell, but then was pulled along with the tide of the others, like a little fish swimming with the current. Most of the party washed up around a large bonfire. Seating herself on a driftwood log, she was overcome with a sense of being adrift from everyone.

They were here. This was when Kit said they were supposed to be having sex, but he was off talking to his new friend. Her heart hurt at the thought that he was more interested in Leo than in her. As the night grew longer, it began to dawn on her that she'd never, ever be enough for Kit because she wasn't what he was looking for. He wanted something that she could never be, and in some ways, that stung more than outright rejection.

Then there was Jack, who sat across from her with his surfer good looks and good-natured personality. Her eyes kept wandering over to him as Nalin played the guitar and everyone else joined in a singalong. Every time she looked over at Jack, he was staring back. She cast him a faint smile.

Alice was getting more attention from him than from her own boyfriend. To be fair, Jack didn't know about Kit. She still hadn't mentioned anything about her relationship, not that he'd asked, and there never seemed to be the right time to do it.

The longer she left it, the more it seemed like she was hiding it from him. Or maybe she was starting to believe the omission. Everyone always mistook them as friends only, and it was always so awkward—so embarrassing—to explain they were actually boyfriend-girlfriend. Kit certainly didn't seem to care about it. He could have said something when Nalin joked. Or done something. All it would have taken was for him to hold her hand. Wasn't that what they were supposed to do anyway?

Everyone else on the beach was so open about touching and kissing the person they were with or flirting with. Kit was the one boy who'd showed any deep interest in her, and she usually found such comfort in that. After a long day that blurred so much of their relationship, things started coming into focus for her.

Having lived her entire fifteen years being compared to her sister, Alice always fell short. Not as smart, not as pretty, not as worth the effort. Even with Kit, when it came to the physical side of their relationship, his attention always seemed elsewhere. But the way Jack looked at her made her think differently. When her gaze fell away to the spot on the beach where Kit and Leo had been, her heart sank. They were gone.

Kit and Leo wandered off along the boardwalk and farther down the beach. String lights hung between poles and tall grass swayed in the ocean breeze as they found their way to a couple of facing benches. They sat on the one with their backs to the path behind them as Kit finished a joke.

"And Dolly Parton comes in and goes: 'I do!'" Kit said, shaking his chest for dramatic effect. "Two of them!"

Leo busted up laughing, composing himself enough to point at Kit and admit, "I have a Dolly Parton poster on my wall."

Kit screwed up his face. "Ewwwww!"

"My brother put it there."

Sensing he'd been too hard on Leo, Kit conceded, "She's really funny."

Leo glanced down, changing topic abruptly. "I like your shoes."

"They're wrecked," Kit lamented again, trying to keep a light tone despite his shoes' shabby appearance.

Eyelids heavy, a wide smile formed on Leo's lips. "I'm a little drunk. Are you?"

"Not really."

"That sucks," he said sadly. After a pause he gestured toward Kit, almost touching his sleeve. "I like your shirt."

"Thanks."

He waited another breath. "Too bad you're not a little drunk."

Eyebrows pinched, Kit asked, "Why's that?"

Leo's words came out in a rushed flow, tumbling out of

him one syllable at a time. "Because sometimes, if you're a little drunk, things happen that sometimes wouldn't if you weren't."

At first not making sense, then piecing the meaning together, Kit let out a little scoff. "Like what?"

Instead of answering Leo changed the topic again. "I like your eyes."

"My eyes?" Kit repeated.

"Can I look at them a bit closer?"

"Okay." Kit smiled anxiously.

Leo leaned forward like he was going to tell a secret. "Closer?"

"Okay."

Leaning in even more, he asked, "Closer?"

At that point, Kit peeked over Leo's shoulder quickly. One of the campfires was just beyond the tall grass. "People can see."

"No, they can't," Leo argued. "Closer?"

Kit nodded, giddy. Now they were close enough to kiss. For a flash of a second, Leo's gaze wavered, and he suddenly shoved Kit away.

"Don't get queer on me, man!" he yelled, getting up and storming away.

"What?" Kit turned in his seat.

"Your boyfriend's a weirdo," Leo accused.

Alice. Standing on the path between the string lights,

her eyes flooded with tears. "He's not my boyfriend," she answered, her voice damp.

She turned quickly and walked away. It really was the end of the world.

# LOVE HURTS

**K**it chased after her, heart and mind racing. His platform shoes clapped on the boardwalk that wound through the rocky shoreline back toward the parking lot as he staggered to catch up, feet sore from walking all day.

"Alice, wait. Alice. Alice!"

At the last loud cry, he glanced over at a group of nearby teens huddled around a fire, hoping they hadn't seen anything and that he wasn't drawing any more unwanted attention to himself. Leo had run off and wasn't among them. That was one thing he could be thankful about in this whole ordeal.

Alice struggled, not sure if she was more angry at herself or at him, and when she heard her name called out that final, desperate time, she finally succumbed to answering without stopping.

"What?" she asked, voice unnervingly still, like the calm before a storm.

She wished she was a bird. Instead, she felt like a cloud, burdened with tears about to rain down. Given the options of fight or flight, her body chose the latter. Her legs kept carrying her away, following the path of the boardwalk.

All the while he kept chasing her. If he didn't stop, she'd have to fight, wouldn't she? But she was so tired.

"Where are you going, Alice?" Kit grasped at words, anything to keep her with him. "Nothing happened. That was—Leo's the weirdo."

He gestured back toward darkness even though her back was to him.

"Is he?" Her tone was so unnervingly cool that it added to Kit's anxiety.

"Yeah," he insisted. "Nothing happened."

"Why are you lying?"

"I'm not lying."

Exasperated, he didn't understand why she wouldn't take him at his word. It wasn't like he'd ever lied to her before. He followed on her heels, clip-clopping in his platform shoes like a wounded horse needing to be put out of its misery.

"Nothing happened," he said.

"Is he a weirdo, Kit? Is Leo a weirdo?"

He floundered. "I don't know."

"Don't lie."

A cold wind came in off the ocean and billowed through his shirt. "I—I'm a little drunk, okay."

Incredulous, she shook her head. Words spat out of her mouth bitterly. "No, you're not."

"Alice, nothing happened."

"You're a liar."

"No, I'm not."

"You're a liar!"

"No, I'm not," he repeated. "I didn't do—"

"You know what?" Her voice broke as tears brimmed in her eyes, but she forced herself to speak, more ferocious with every syllable. "Some people are lucky and some people are unlucky and some people are goddamn liars."

With that, she marched past him, back toward the crowd by the campfire. There was more safety in numbers and he wouldn't want to make a scene.

"Alice . . ."

"Go to hell," she told him as she brushed by.

Kit didn't have the strength to follow as his own emotions bubbled up, threatening to spill out. Although he struggled to contain it, a sob escaped, and he tilted his head back, eyes closed, trying to get a grip.

Alice strode back through the tall grass, onto the rocks, and back toward the beach party. There were too many things racing through her head for her to process. The whole day had felt like one long argument. Now the fuel in her tank had burned down and she was running on fumes. Her entire world was filled with one disappointment after another. Parents hollering at each other so much that it had splintered apart their twenty-year marriage. A sister who was completely oblivious to the shadow she had cast on Alice her entire life. And now Kit. Her best friend in the world. Her boyfriend, who had said he loved her only a few hours ago.

She knew what she'd seen: the anticipation on his face of kissing a boy. He'd never looked at her in that way before. Why had he never looked at her in that way before? He had made things much, much worse by not admitting to what he'd just done. Had he misled her this whole time? She'd seen Kit drunk. Drunk Kit danced without a care in the world with well-practiced moves like he was on *Soul Train*. Of all things, she'd never thought of him as disloyal. Not only had he wanted that kiss, he'd been quick to throw Leo to the wolves, calling him the weirdo.

At a small campfire ahead, the group was dispersing, Jack among them. He looked around as if searching for something he'd lost, and when he caught sight of her he brightened, waving.

Taking a moment to pull herself together, using her too-long cardigan sleeves to wipe her eyes, she made her way toward him. The others were wandering off toward the bigger bonfire. With every step Alice took, a boldness began to take over where grief and anger had been just moments ago.

By the time she reached him, her eyes were dry. She regained her composure enough that he couldn't tell anything was wrong, or at least he didn't let on if he did. Jack gestured down at a beach blanket, and they hunkered down together. Reaching into a cooler, he cracked open a beer and handed it to her before grabbing one for himself.

"Thanks."

She took a big drink for added courage and then another for good measure. Spilling slightly, Alice wiped her lips before setting the bottle down in the sand beside her. On her other side, Jack shifted closer, and when she glanced over at him, he was looking directly at her. Head angled over his shoulder, the firelight cast shadows over his chiselled features.

He was a cute boy who liked her in a way that Kit obviously didn't. Her sister Denise didn't know what she was missing. Sometimes she was too smart for her own good, choosing books over boys. Something that Nalin had said earlier stuck with her.

With a coy smile, she leaned forward. "So, you really think I'm prettier than my sister?"

His eyes searched hers. "Yeah."

For once when being compared to her sister, Alice came out on the winning side. She stared at Jack, turning her body toward his and gazing straight into his eyes. "You never had a chance with her."

It was a little mean but it was a gambit.

With a little sigh, he admitted, "Yeah, I know."

Her face softened as she added, "But you do with me."

And she kissed him. Jack reciprocated tenderly, leaning into it and gently nibbling her bottom lip. Every part of her was alive and tingling. Jack kissed her like she'd never been kissed before. His strong hands caressed her, fingers squeezing the flesh on her sides and all the way up her back.

She responded in kind, hands running across his wide shoulders. Swept away in the moment, one of his hands slipped beneath the hem of her T-shirt. The warmth of it was a sweet surprise in the cold night air. Yet as much as she enjoyed the thrill of it, she pulled back.

"Am I going too fast?" he asked.

Although she wasn't sure they were, she nodded because it was probably better to err on the side of caution. The one thing she was certain about in that moment was she didn't want to regret her first time. He brushed her hair back, tucking a strand behind her ear and pressing a kiss against her eyebrow.

"How are you getting back?"

The words brought back the day's earlier conversation with Kit. He had wanted to use Alice getting home as an excuse for her to not come with him. She had suspected it then, but knew it for a fact now. How different things might have gone if she hadn't insisted on going to Dominion Beach.

Alice shrugged. "Same as how I got here."

"Hitchhiking? Is that safe?"

"I can take care of myself."

With a grin, Jack said, "I don't doubt it. Let me give you a ride though. I want to make sure you get home okay."

"Why?" she asked, more because she wanted him to say the words out loud. "You don't even really know me."

"Because," he said, "I want to change that."

Alice struggled not to grin as she shook her head. She wasn't declining just because she was afraid of dying in a car wreck. Some little part of her felt beholden to Kit even in spite of what had happened just then. She would see him to his mom's place before leaving. Maybe they would find a way to make things right before she left. Or at least less wrong.

"I told Kit I'd go with him to his mom's place."

"You're a good friend," he noted. Then he leaned forward so they could kiss again. It was just as passionate as the first time, only he kept his hands above her shirt.

Kit had finally summoned the strength to follow her. Now he watched from a distance, pained at the thought of losing her, knowing there was absolutely nothing he could do about it. Like a ghost, he wandered farther down the beach. Everyone was too drunk and stoned to notice him. They looked right through him.

Even if he wanted to, he couldn't rejoin the party. He was too sober and way too mixed up, and the one person he would have turned to for help was the very one he had inadvertently wronged. If he was being honest with himself and with her, he had wanted Leo to kiss him. Wanted it more than he'd ever wanted to kiss Alice.

The long night couldn't end soon enough. He found an abandoned beach blanket to lie on and tried to sleep with his suitcase as a pillow. With his arms folded across his chest to keep warm, he closed his eyes, huddled by a fire. Somewhere he overheard Marylou and Jeanie having a drunken argument.

"He said he liked me."

"He said he liked both of us."

Of course he liked Alice, everyone should like Alice, Kit thought. She was the coolest girl around, everyone else just needed to catch up to Kit's way of thinking. He hoped she would know it, too, and that Jack wasn't going to break her heart for a second time that night. As much as that thought bothered Kit, she was free to do with her heart whatever she wanted.

"But you said you didn't like him."

"'Cause I didn't think he liked me."

"You can't just like somebody because they like you."

"Yes, you can."

"Frig off!" That must have been Jeanie. "No, you can't."

"That's exactly why anybody likes anybody."

In that moment he wanted to shut them out. If only his problems were as simple as theirs. Not everyone was free to like whomever they chose. Leo had made that abundantly clear. Kit wished he was a normal teenage boy, that his worst life issues were on par with the average high-school teen, openly arguing about crushes. He cringed at the idea of Leo telling the others about what had happened between him and Kit.

It was the first time he'd ever come close to kissing a boy. Before then, he wasn't even sure if he really wanted to. Or at least that's what he'd told himself. By middle school, when other boys started pairing off with girls, he'd begun to feel awkward and inferior because he had no interest in doing the same.

Then two summers ago he'd been sent away to camp as part of his dad's attempt to give him a "normal" childhood. Kit knew it even then. Maybe his dad could tell Kit wasn't turning out the way he was supposed to and figured he just needed to learn how to be a boy. Trouble was, there was a camp counsellor who was the spitting image of teen heartthrob Donny Osmond. Every time he came near him, Kit would blush and his palms would sweat.

That was the first time he heard the insults—queer, pansy, and so on. He didn't understand the words then, just that they were bad. So he tried to shut it all out and forget about the feelings he had for the older boy. He wasn't even sure what they meant. But the names followed him back to school and he couldn't escape the stigma of who he might be.

Then toward the end of this school semester, Alice kissed him. In a lot of ways, it was a safe kiss because she was his best friend. Besides, even though she was a girl, Alice wasn't like other girls. His spirit animal was right: she looked a little butch. Maybe that's why it didn't feel completely wrong. But it *was* wrong. And now he didn't know how to make it right again.

Someone hurled something into one of the fires behind him, startling him. The sound of flames engulfed the object. He squeezed his eyes shut but it was no use. Between the ruckus around him and the all-consuming void of emotion inside, he couldn't sleep.

Kit stared at the fire in front of him, watching the wood burn down and listening to the flames crackle. All he wished for that night was to burn away the day. *Unlucky*.

# YOU'RE SO VAIN

In the morning Alice sat on the quiet beach and hugged her knees to her chest. The tide was out and muddy flats spread out in front of her, beyond which the sun rose over the ocean. Debris littered the beach. The campfires had long since burned out.

In that moment she knew that even if she somehow never saw Jack again, even if Kit was telling the truth about what had happened on the boardwalk, it was over between them. She wasn't sure if it had ever truly begun. Maybe she'd been running with the idea of being in a relationship with Kit for so long that she'd never stopped to think he wasn't in the race with her. A part of her must have known all along. But she still loved him in a way. Otherwise she would have left with Jack.

A crow flew high above. She followed its path off into the distance until it landed on a church steeple. It amazed her how quiet and at peace everything could be at this hour.

Shivering in the early morning air, she drew herself into her cardigan. The party goers had cleared out hours ago, returning to their respective homes. In their wake broken folding chairs and bottles were scattered across the beach.

Kit's sleep had been fitful, and he'd been sure he was going to wake up alone, cold and abandoned on the beach. But when he woke up, combing sand out of his hair with his fingertips, he smiled over at her as though nothing had happened.

It filled her with such regret that she had to look away. Alice could hardly believe how difficult it was—to be in a relationship with someone who was lying to himself just as much as she'd been lying to herself. That part was almost laughable, if it wasn't so damn sad.

"I gotta find a bathroom," she told him.

"There's one in that store over there, I think," Kit said, pointing beyond the parking lot.

She glanced over briefly to see where he was pointing.

"I gotta wash my hair," Kit added with a laugh, then asked, "Do you have to wash your hair?"

"No."

"You can use my blow-dryer," he offered, as if that was the only thing holding her back from using a bathroom sink to wash up.

She turned to him slowly. "You brought your blow-dryer?"

"Yeah." He patted his hair down.

With a heavy sigh she said, "Of course you did."

"I am a weirdo," he noted lightly, like it was a joke.

She nodded, giving him a half smile. "Yeah."

With that Alice rose, taking her satchel with her as she left Kit lying on the beach. Gently, Andy Warhol leaned his shoulder into his and they both watched her walk away.

"I'm a weirdo," Kit repeated for his benefit.

"Oh, honey. She's a weirdo, too," Andy Warhol observed, reassuringly. "We're all weirdos. That's what makes us beautiful."

Kit scoffed.

"I love this T-shirt!" Andy Warhol exclaimed as he picked the discarded item up from the sand.

As he held it up, Kit recognized it as his favourite Edward Bear T-shirt. He hadn't even noticed she'd taken it off. Or maybe he had but wanted to pretend he hadn't, because of what it meant.

"Can I have it?"

"Sure."

Andy Warhol got to his feet and wandered off. Picking up his suitcase, Kit left the beach to catch up with Alice on the boardwalk.

In the washroom of the general store he washed up, wetting his hair in the sink then using the blow-dryer to restyle it. After, he changed into his polka-dot shirt with the wide collar and a pair of plaid pants. It was an outfit he never would have worn back home, but he felt more comfortable having seen how people had dressed the night before.

He found Alice outside at a picnic table eating chips. She had only changed out of her top and into a cotton peasant shirt. Wordlessly, he offered her his blow-dryer so she could at least wash her hair but she shook her head. Rolling her eyes as he stowed it away in his suitcase, Alice got up.

She looked back to make sure he was following. As they began the walk back into the city, Alice watched a couple stroll by. The man's arm was around the woman's shoulders and the way they looked at each other made it seem as though nothing else in the world mattered. She used to think it was such a simple thing, to love and to be loved. Now she knew better. There were many nuances that she never imagined, and love was a minefield of heartache.

They passed by a church where a motley choir sang, and then Kit led the way through a graveyard that overlooked the city. A field of grave markers stretched out before a panoramic view of Sydney. Careful about where she was stepping, Alice followed him, thinking at first that they were taking a shortcut to his mom's place.

In the middle of the graveyard was a two-tiered stone planter. It had a circular base several metres wide, and was elaborately carved. The only thing growing in it was grass. Kit sat on the edge, taking in the view. For a moment, Alice stared at him, not really interested in prolonging their little misadventure. Grabbing what she needed from her satchel, she set it down then took a seat next to him. After sparking up a cigarette, she tossed her lighter down by her bag.

"Why are we here?" she asked.

"In Sydney?"

"No," she stated. "In this stupid graveyard."

He pursed his lips. Even though he wanted to talk to her about what had happened last night, he didn't have the right words. Alice was looking up, hands resting in the crook between her knees.

"I know why we're in stupid Sydney," she continued, flippant. "We're in stupid Sydney so I could make you fall in love with me so you wouldn't move here."

"I do love you, Alice."

"No, you don't," she retorted, voice full of accusation.

"I'm not a liar."

What he felt for Alice was unlike anything he felt for anyone else in his life. She was special in a way he couldn't quite place. If he was lying about that, he was lying to himself, not just to her.

She took a drag. "Everybody's a liar."

They looked down in silence. If what she said was true, he wondered what she had lied about to him.

"I always knew you didn't want to kiss me when you kissed me," Alice told him.

"I wanted to," he insisted.

She didn't respond, just continued drawing from her cigarette.

"I wanted to want to," he amended, the truth being pulled from him like the nicotine from her smoke. In a way, it felt like he was poisoning himself. In another way, it was a sweet rush of air after holding his breath for so long.

After another pause, Alice exhaled. "Are you gay?"

She looked over her shoulder at him. His hands were clasped together tightly and he had a pained look on his face. If he lied to her again, she promised herself she'd leave right then and there.

"'Cause if you are, you have to say it," Alice commanded. "You have to say it out loud."

With a succinct nod Kit said, "I am."

The heavy weight finally lifted between them. Alice breathed deeply.

"I really wish I wasn't though," he added. "It would make everything easier."

"No, it wouldn't."

Her voice was full of disbelief at his naïveté. It was so easy to discredit, but she didn't understand how hard it was to recognize that every day for the rest of his life someone would be judging him. She hadn't wanted him to move away, didn't understand how their small town would suffocate him.

"You know, I kind of thought you knew maybe."

She let out a long sigh, dusting ashes off her pant leg. "Yeah, maybe I kind of did."

"I do love you, Alice." It was important that she knew. "Forever and for always."

"You'll forget you even said that."

"No, I won't." Suddenly he reached up and pressed two fingers to his forehead. "I'm touching my third eye."

"That's how you remember moments," he explained fervently. "Y-you touch your third eye to wake it up a-and you'll always remember that moment. My mom told me. Try it out."

The earnest way he spoke only illustrated how vastly far apart they were about everything. She pressed her eyes shut to push back tears, head shaking almost imperceptibly as he spoke. They were no longer boyfriend-girlfriend. After months of fooling herself into thinking he was into her, it was over. All that was left was the sting of how it ended. How were they supposed to move forward when he wanted to keep this memory alive?

When he was done with his hippie-dippy bullcrap, she took a calming breath then told him, "I don't want to remember this."

His hand dropped abruptly as his heart sank. After all that, she still didn't believe him—didn't believe how dear she was to him. But maybe it was more than that. Maybe she didn't want to remember what they once were because it reminded her of her hurt and anger. He did that to her. And there was no undoing it.

They sat side by side in silence, staring out at the view of Sydney spread before them. A cloud of nicotine blew over his face as Alice finished what seemed like the longest cigarette ever.

# STARSHIP TROOPER

**K**it had imagined his mom living someplace cool. Maybe not a factory like Andy Warhol, but a studio flat or some other elegant setup. Instead he wound his way through a quiet residential neighbourhood. They slowed their pace as they passed two huge hosta plants and approached an old Victorian house shaded by an ancient oak tree out front.

As Kit took the five steps up to the door, he noticed the crumbling paint on the decorative moulding around the frames of the door and windows. Even the carved stone banister was chipping with age. He knocked firmly, but there was no immediate answer. After waiting for a few seconds, he turned his head down, listening for sounds within.

Meanwhile, Alice stood back, looking around and trying to peer in the front window. Bending over, Kit peeped through the mail slot. Then he held his ear against the door once more before knocking again. The sound of music from out back caught their attention.

"Come on," she said, motioning for Kit to join her.

He moved past the open wrought-iron gate and led the way through a backyard that was overgrown and wild. Bushes of flowering peonies and other foliage crowded around the narrow path. It was a fragrant, suburban jungle. They had to duck and push past it all until it finally opened up to a patch of mowed lawn by a wood deck.

With every step forward, Kit's anticipation almost got the better of him. He wanted to race to his mom the way he had when he was a little boy, but thought it too undignified. It had been so long since he'd last seen her that a flood of images and memories rushed through his mind, making it impossible to hold on to any one in particular. And then there she was, like a dream come to life.

Kit stopped suddenly in front of Alice so she had to peer around him to see anything. His mother stood, a statuesque woman in her early forties, barefoot on the grass. She wore a white gown with cut-out shoulders, one hand in the air and the other at her throat. Her eyes were closed and her head was tossed back. With her hair done up loosely, she looked like something out of a Waterhouse painting.

When the beat picked up in the rock song blaring from a nearby boom box, his mother came to life. She began to move, graceful and airy in stark contrast to the music. Kit watched, completely enthralled, as she swayed and twirled toward him. She threw an arm back and opened her eyes. Her jaw dropped at the sight of him.

"Oh, baby," she said to Kit. "Honey. You're here."

His mom ran to him, took his face in her hands, and kissed him on the cheek.

"Yeah." He laughed as he spoke. The scent of her eau de toilette was precisely how he remembered it. Floral and fruity with spicy undertones. Singulier by Pierre Cardin. With the smell came memories of watching his mother's makeup routine in the bathroom. He'd sit on the closed toilet lid that had a decorative carpet cover and watch her transform into her other self, the one that went to fancy parties.

Applying powder to hold the colours in place always marked that she was done with her makeup application, at which point Kit would stand on the toilet because she'd spray the perfume into the air between them and walk, eyes closed, into the mist. Her eyes would open just as she reached him and she'd deliver a kiss to his forehead. The scent of her would hang on him, on his pillow and clothes, long after she was gone.

While her hands lingered around his neckline, she took note of Alice behind him. "Is this your girlfriend?"

"No," Alice answered quickly.

"Best friend," Kit said overtop of her.

"I'm Alice."

"Alice," she repeated dreamily. "Alice? Did you bring my boy to me?"

Before Alice could answer, Kit's mother grabbed her and pulled her into a similar embrace.

"I guess," Alice managed to say.

Kit's mom cupped her hands around Alice's face and pressed a kiss onto her cheek. Then she stared into her eyes and simultaneously brought one hand back over to Kit's cheek, beaming at them both. Speechless, Kit's mom took one big step back. With her hands over her mouth, she took them both in, completely breathless. As if suddenly inspired, she clapped her hands together.

"Let's make sandwiches."

"Yeah," Kit agreed. "Come on."

His mom hiked her long skirt up and skipped up the porch steps.

"Come on!" Kit said to Alice as he followed, excited.

Trailing slightly behind them, Alice moved past the boom box on a table with a stack of eight-track cassettes and a near-empty fancy glass of port by a ceramic ashtray. It wasn't even noon yet. It was possible that Kit's mom simply led such a bohemian lifestyle that she didn't know what time of day it was. Alice wanted to give her the benefit of the doubt, if only for Kit's sake. He had pinned so many of his hopes on this invitation to live with his mother that it would shatter his world to discover what everyone in town said about her was true.

Kit urged Alice to join them inside, so she followed cautiously. They made their way into an eclectic kitchen from another era. The cupboards had no doors, exposing shelves piled with mismatched dishes and lots of packaged foods containing an odd assortment of things. Tins of spam were stacked next to something called *mejillones en escabeche* beside which was a vat of cherries. There were no signs of fresh produce. The air was filled with the chemical scents of paints and thinners with a hint of burned toast. They sat at the enormous kitchen table while his mom spread out ingredients to make sandwiches on the counter. She took out a package of sliced deli meat and a jar of mayonnaise from the fridge, then proceeded to hack thick wedges of bread.

"I love your house," Kit said.

"Isn't it wonderful!" His mother made big gestures when she spoke, going back and forth between making them lunch and talking grandly. "I share it with a couple of other artists—Jim and Alejandro."

At that point she brought the board onto the table so she could talk and prep at the same time. She gesticulated while holding a serrated knife, and Alice was glad to be seated on the other side of the wide country-kitchen table lest she be skewered.

"And I've been painting. I'll show you." Laura put a piece of cheese in Kit's mouth like he was a toddler and he laughed as he let her. "My rooms are at the top of the stairs. The whole third floor is studios. It's fantastic. You should go look around."

Her arms flew up in the air as she described her home like she lived and breathed every word of it. Kit was enamoured with it all, soaking in every bit of what she was saying.

"In a minute."

Shifting uncomfortably in her seat, Alice rubbed her arm and glanced around the kitchen. The countertop was cluttered with items that didn't belong in a kitchen, including glasses filled with coloured water and paintbrushes. A huge bag of plaster of Paris sat next to the breadbox and could easily be mistaken for flour. Alice wondered how many sips of diluted paint had been drunk and loaves of plaster bread had been made by accident.

Exploring the house was the perfect excuse for Alice to leave them to catch up.

"I'll go look around," she said, getting up.

"Go, darling," Kit's mother insisted, flourishing her hands majestically. "Explore."

Before Alice had even left the room, he asked, "Can I turn on your radio?"

His mother let out an exclamation of joy. "If music be the food of love, play on!"

Alice heard the radio switch on as she wandered off. Their conversation continued as she stepped into the hallway, a ghost haunting the place, unseen. The walls were covered with art, both paintings and photographs, and reflected the different styles of the three artists who shared the space.

One was distinctly pop art using a mix of comics, print ads, and pop culture items that Kit would love. Another took pieces of mail and repurposed them into collages using postcards, rubber stamps, paint, and other images. The third artist worked exclusively in paint. Alice figured this art belonged to Kit's mom, and not just because the woman had said as much in the kitchen. While some of her paintings were done in vivid colours, others were quite dark, but all shared a raw and untamed quality.

Ever so slowly, Alice made her way up a grand staircase, pausing to poke her head up past the banister. The stairs wound up and up and up. Along the way she took in all the strange and beautiful pieces lining the walls. She had been to the Art Gallery of Nova Scotia in Halifax on a school trip once. Unlike a gallery where space was given between pieces, everything here was pressed against each other, sometimes overlapping. It was overwhelming and hard to focus on any one artwork.

She passed room upon room filled with art and worn furniture that had seen better days, likely hand-me-downs,

thrift-shop purchases, or collected from curbsides. Bohemian and starving artist all at once, it reeked of struggle
and sadness. At the top of the stairs, Alice entered Kit's
mom's room, the doors already open in welcome.

The small bedroom was sparsely furnished with a single bed and plain linens. A wall closet was crammed full
of clothes and shoes. Past a drawn curtain divider was
her studio. Alice walked beyond the threshold where a
curio stood. It was filled with all sorts of knick-knacks but
mostly clusters of ornate cocktail glasses. A shimmering
gold eye mask was propped up in a ceramic cup.

Absently, she ran her fingers through a bowl of sea-
shells. Pinned along the back of the middle shelf were
photos of Kit's mom from when she was younger. In one
she was dressed in her wedding gown. There were small
canvasses scattered around the shelves. Alice got a sense
that they were self-portraits, only they didn't have any
faces. The paintings were just swirling lines that took the
shape of a woman. One was a silhouette, but black on the
outside. The darkness of the surroundings bled into the
pure white on the inside. It unnerved her.

When she turned to examine the rest of the room, Alice
folded one arm across her chest and put a hand to her
mouth to brace herself against the frenzied chaos of it. A
large table was filled with small cans of paint, in front of
which paintings were stacked against each other maybe

ten deep. Alice knelt to inspect the outermost one more closely. The large painting made little sense to her but it was signed, so presumably complete. As she bent down, she felt a warm light on her coming in through the pale drapes.

Turning around again, a huge canvas caught her eye. This one was a work in progress. A drop cloth was spread out on the floor beneath it, where more cans of paint and brushes awaited the artist. Alice stood before it, drawn to this piece more than any of the others. The canvas was overrun with colours, as if the paint had been thrown rather than brushed on.

The painting reminded Alice of stars blinking in the night sky. There were so many little specks of them. What did any one of them even matter when they were all jumbled together like that? Even a shooting star was only noticed for a second. And only then by those who were actually looking.

It was like what Andy Warhol said about fifteen minutes of fame. Of course, that made her think of Kit and how she was just one little star fading out from his life. Tears welled in her eyes. And she stood there for a very long time, trying to make sense of it all. How could anyone be lucky when the odds were so stacked against them?

Eventually, she made her way back downstairs. The giddy voices of Kit and his mom travelled down the hallway above the music. Alice stood at kitchen door, peering in to watch him teaching his mom some dance moves.

" . . . so he would usually be like something like this and she would do like up," he instructed.

They moved their hands in the air and shook their hips as he spoke. The woman had tucked the middle of her skirt in to the elastic of her panties right at the thigh so as to shorten the length.

"Yeah!" he said. "Let's try it. Okay. One, two, three, go!"

"Spin!" his mom added as she twirled around.

In the kitchen of an old Victorian house, Kit and his mom danced to disco music. They were having the time of their lives, feet clapping on the hardwood floor while they snapped their fingers to keep time.

Head down, Alice swept by them and out the back door. She stepped into the garden and shut the door behind her; the laughter inside made her look back once or twice. Making her way to the wrought-iron gate, all she could think of were the stars blinking out at night. Who would ever notice if one went out completely?

# WHITE RABBIT

**W**hen the back door opened and shut again, Alice noted the music had stopped. If Kit was going to try to stop her, she wouldn't hear him out. He was here, now with his mom, having fulfilled the only part of their weekend plans he had intended to. She owed him nothing.

"Where are you going?" Kit's mom called in an ethereal voice.

Hands clasped around the straps of her satchel, Alice stopped to look back and found the woman standing on tiptoe at edge of the porch, as if the grass were lava.

"Don't run away, Alice!" she said airily. "Come back in to Wonderland and have your sandwich."

Kit's mom clutched her skirt in front of her, giggling and smiling. The promise of real food made Alice hesitate—the bag of chips from this morning had all but disappeared from her stomach, and in that hungry moment she couldn't think of an excuse to leave. It wasn't like she had a ride lined up, and Kit's mom was just standing there, warm and inviting, the anticipation on her face so earnest that Alice second-guessed everything.

Just because Kit and she weren't a couple didn't mean her relationship with him was blinking out. Maybe it was becoming something else, the way a star could turn into a red giant. And maybe that was better because that was how things were supposed to be.

"Come on," the woman insisted with her hands held out as if to a small child.

Alice succumbed, giving her a weak smile as she walked back up to the porch.

Kit's mom took her by the hand and led her back inside. "Aren't you hungry?" she asked softly. "You must be *so* hungry."

The way the woman spoke to her made Alice feel like she was the only thing that was important in that moment. With all the rumours in town, Kit's mom must have known what it was like to be on the outside, and so here she was, extending an invitation for Alice to join their inner circle. Sweet and tender and genuine. Alice wanted to be wrapped in that kindness. It made her understand Kit's desire to come here in the first place.

Once inside, Kit pulled her down beside him and they ate their sandwiches while his mom took a call from the wall phone. At the table, Kit flipped through a photo album with pictures of his mother from when she was younger and a model in Toronto. It showcased different styles through her career, from mod to hippie. One series of photos was taken outside the Art Gallery of Ontario and there was a particular wildness about her that was oddly compelling.

Kit's mom whispered into the phone with her forehead pressed into the corner between the wall and cupboard. In an almost sensual way she stroked a tea towel that was thrown over her shoulder. The whole display was distracting to Alice, who toyed with the tassels on her peasant blouse as her eyes wandered between her friend and his mom. Alice smiled over at Kit, then glanced surreptitiously past him.

The woman's entire demeanour had changed from only a few moments ago. Her body language was closed off now, like she was trying to block out the rest of the world except for whoever was on the phone. Kit was too absorbed by the photos to notice his mom's behaviour. Even when she hung up abruptly, slamming the receiver down and strutting back into their full view, he didn't think to ask her if anything was the matter.

"Tell Alice about meeting Andy Warhol!"

"Oh!" She twirled back around, flinging the tea towel in the air and smiling girlishly before replacing the cloth on her shoulder. "Andy was delightful! What a party. They took over the whole hotel."

Alice started to see links form, like in one of those connect-the-dot puzzles. Somehow, Andy Warhol was the line that drew Kit and his mom together. She'd heard Kit tell this particular story before and only half believed the details that he swore up and down were the truth. To hear it from the source would be quite the show, given Laura's flair for dramatics.

"Kit said he took your picture," Alice noted, trying to sound encouraging.

"He did," he insisted.

His mom picked up a lit cigarette and held it between her fingers as she waved her hand dramatically. The top of her dress was askew, falling off one shoulder. "Andy was *always* taking pictures!"

"Tell her."

Indulging Kit, she posed as she told the story, eyelashes batting. "It was Toronto. And they showed their films and we *all* went, and there was this—this party . . . in this *decrepit* hotel."

Staring off into nothing, she lost herself deep in the memory. Kit was completely entranced by her performance—at least, that's what it was to Alice, a show Laura was putting on for her son. They fed off each other, the way he encouraged her storytelling and she acted out the part of socialite.

"There were rooms there that were just filled with silver balloons!" she exclaimed, gesturing high above her head as if they were right there in front of them. "There was one room with mounds of dirt."

"Dirt?" Alice repeated.

"Mounds of dirt growing *daffodils*." Kit's mom giggled while her fingers flowed as if she were interpreting her words into a sign language of her own design. The next part she acted out as if in a play. "And shirtless waiters with astronaut helmets carrying trays of manhattans."

Her hands went down her body suggestively to imply nakedness, then she put on an imaginary helmet and propped up invisible trays on either side of her head. The story was full of such strange detail, but one was missing.

"When was this?" Alice asked.

"A million years ago," Laura answered, melancholy dripping from her voice as she pulled the tea towel from her shoulder and rolled her eyes.

"Where was Kit?"

The question surprised his mom, taking her out of the moment. She had to dig for the answer and it came out flat and uninteresting compared to her tall tale. "Kit was a baby. He was at home. I'd gone away for a while."

Kit nodded in approval.

"Why?"

"Because sometimes people have to go away," she explained matter of factly yet somewhat put out as she drew on her cigarette and turned her eyes to the floor.

"Was Mr. Morash there?"

"Are you an inquisitor?" Laura retorted, one hand on hip, eyes squinting.

Alice took her hands off the table and sat back a bit.

With a smile, Kit picked up the story. "Andy asked you to come to New York."

"He did, he did," his mom agreed. "He said . . . 'come to New York.'"

She leaned forward to tap her ashes into a tray on the kitchen table.

"He did?" Alice asked, unconvinced.

"Alice!" Kit's mom cried abruptly.

With that outburst Alice thought she'd be scolded again, but the woman put on a playful expression.

"Alice . . . in Wonderland."

"Yeah."

Alice smiled but it didn't reach her eyes. It was an old joke that she had grown tired of in her fifteen years. Moreover, she was growing increasingly alarmed by Kit's mother's manic behaviour.

"Down the rabbit hole!" the woman added harshly.

Again, she acted out her next words, stretching out tall with a booming voice to say, "This one makes you bigger!"

Then huddling down with a shrinking voice to finish, "This one makes you small . . ."

"I wasn't named for the story," Alice interrupted. "My grandmother was Alice."

All she could see of Kit's mom was her eyes as the woman hunkered on the other side of the table beyond a cluster of dishes and sandwich ingredients that had yet to be put away.

"Was she evil?" the woman asked as she stood slowly and drew a puff from her cigarette.

"No."

"Grandmothers often are," she warned, exhaling a long trail of smoke.

Confused, Alice said, "I thought that was stepmothers."

"*And* grandmothers," his mom insisted.

Kit tried changing tack. "You know what I decided? I think I'm going to learn how to play the piano."

The announcement garnered no response from his mom, who continued to level a cool gaze at his friend.

So Alice informed him, "Guitars are cooler than pianos."

"No, they're not." He was annoyed by her persistent negativity.

She didn't care. "Yes, they are."

He raised his palms as he gave proof positive. "Elton John plays piano."

It was actually a relief to Alice that he'd changed topics and shifted the focus away from her, so she let it go.

Whatever it was that she'd done to set off his mom was something she'd try to avoid doing again before she left. Instead, she continued down the clear path that Kit had presented. Parents were supposed to have some kind of inherent interest in hearing about what kids dreamed of doing, especially when it came to the when-I-grow-up variety of ambitions.

"I decided I want to be a cop," Alice announced, nodding proudly.

"What?" His mom put hand to her own throat, staring at the girl as though she'd spoken an unfamiliar foreign language.

"A . . . police officer."

The woman's eyes shifted back and forth for a moment, like a spring had snapped within her. Then she stamped out her cigarette harshly in the ashtray.

"I will not have it," she declared, taking a massive step back to glare at Kit for having brought this intruder into her home. "I will *not*!"

With that, the woman flapped her tea towel at her son and stormed out of the room. Not knowing what else to do, Kit rose from his seat and chased after her. Left confused and alone, Alice glanced down at the open photo album at a head shot with a black background. In it Kit's mom stared off at some distant point, like she was lost.

After a moment, Alice wandered out of the kitchen and

headed back toward the staircase. From the patter of footsteps she could hear Kit and Laura ascending toward her rooms. Alice took a tentative step up, peering up uselessly.

"Mom!"

"I will not have a cop in my house."

"She's not a cop."

"That's what they all say."

"Mom, she's a kid, okay?" Kit reasoned. "She's my age. We go to school together."

A door upstairs slammed violently. While Alice was taking another furtive step, a door at the base of the stairs opened as one of the roommates came out to investigate the noise. Startled at the sight of, Alice, a look of fright crossed his face as he backed into his room and shut his door. Alice didn't blame him.

Upstairs, Kit knocked on the closed door. "Mom!"

"No!"

Alice perched at the bottom of the stairs and craned her neck up, gazing into the darkness above. There was no leaving now. Having fallen down the rabbit hole, all she could do at this point was wait until she hit the bottom.

# CHERRY BOMB

**K**it coaxed and cajoled his mother. Although she couldn't hear all the words, the whispers through the door upstairs made Alice sleepy, and exhaustion eventually took hold. After the emotional and physical tolls of the past day, the low voices above were like the sound of an ocean carrying her away to sleep.

Alice startled when a hand touched her shoulder. On the step beside her, Kit stood smiling down at her. She couldn't tell if he was putting on a brave face or not—with everything that had just happened, she wouldn't hold it against him if he was shaken.

"Come on," he said, his pleasant expression not faltering for even a moment.

Rising to her feet, she hobbled behind with a leg made stiff from being folded beneath her for too long. She was so eager to leave that she almost bumped into him on her way to the kitchen to grab her satchel. But instead of heading out that way, Kit stopped in his tracks, then travelled down the hall in the opposite direction, peering around in search of something.

He let out a little exclamation when he found what he was looking for and disappeared into a room. With tentative steps, Alice followed him just past the doorway and into a dimly lit living room. Blocking natural light from coming in, the ferns and gnarled vines in pots on the windowsill gave even more of a sense of a jungle than the backyard had.

All Alice could think was, "Twas brillig, and the slithy toves / Did gyre and gimble in the wabe." It was complete lunacy, his mother thinking Alice was an actual cop. What other nonsense would Kit have to deal with if he stayed with his mom? The woman was fighting a battle with a Jabberwock of her own imagining, and was completely unarmed against it.

Desk lamps on haphazardly placed end tables had been left on throughout the room. Kit turned on the television and flipped through the channels until he found one with the American Bicentennial parade coverage on it. He seated himself on a worn couch of embroidered mustard-yellow damask. A pair of mismatched chairs—one a cozy rocker, the other a straight-back wood armchair—and a simple coffee table rounded out the collection of furniture in this room.

When he motioned for her to join him, she moved slowly to the couch. Planting herself by his side, Alice wasn't exactly sure what was going on, and she was a little afraid to ask. Was his mom okay? Was he?

As he settled in, she continued scanning the room. A corner bookshelf brimmed with titles. Some kind of colourful cubist painting hung over the television in front of them. Kit was transfixed by the TV screen as he grabbed a handful of peanuts from a bowl on the coffee table.

"Do you want to stay?" Alice asked quietly.

"What are you talking about? Yes!"

He was acting like the whole thing never happened. Like his mom didn't have a meltdown in the kitchen over thinking Alice was actually a cop and not just Kit's fifteen-year-old best friend. They'd both witnessed it, and now he was pretending everything was fine.

Sitting back munching, he added, "You can go if you want to."

Even though she did want to go, she wasn't about to leave him here. At least, not until she was sure he'd be okay. So she shook her head and waved him off, trying to appear as nonchalant as he was.

"I'll wait for a while," she offered. "Just in case."

He took his eyes off the screen. "Just in case what?"

How could she answer that question without point-ing out the obvious truth that Kit was avoiding? The last thing she wanted was to hurt him or, for that matter, see him get hurt, no matter what had happened on the beach. Her life was easy compared to this kind of chaos.

"Nothing," she backpedalled. "Just—I'll wait."

They turned their attention to the TV, where people dressed in triangular hats and period costumes were transporting the Liberty Bell. The announcer said, "*I need not remind you that independence was declared in Philadelphia but that the Liberty Bell was safe. The death toll of the Liberty Bell was almost sounded when in 1777 the big bronze crier was not allowed to stay in the lofty towers of Independence Hall because Congress, fearing that the British were about to attack Philadelphia, ordered it removed . . .*"

At that moment, Kit's mom appeared. She'd put on a shimmering gold, floor-length sheath dress that reminded Alice of Ginger from *Gilligan's Island*. With a great flourish, Laura made an extravagant entrance into the living room. Stopping to stand directly in front of the TV, she raised her free hand toward the ceiling and tilted her head up, then, bringing her open palm to her shoulder, her gaze tracked down toward them.

With a sultry twitch of her shoulder, she giggled and pointed to a tray of drinks held high in her other hand. "These are manhattans and they come in their very own glass."

As she lowered the tray and set drinks in front of them

on the coffee table, she explained, "It's not really a man-hattan if it doesn't come in its own special glass. Just like us. People. We all come in our own special glass. Unless you don't. Then you don't."

She bent her hand at the wrist as if to bat away the last idea. Plunking the tray down with a clang, Kit's mom hiked her skirt up and sat in the rocker, moving to and fro in its sway. Alice didn't say anything, just stared. Even though she wanted to remind the woman they weren't of legal drinking age, she was too afraid she'd set Laura off again. It was something a cop would say. And it would take Kit another half hour to talk sense into her.

Neither one of them touched their drinks right away, so Kit's mom held her glass up and said, "Cheers."

Only then did they oblige. When Kit put his lips to his glass and swallowed a big gulp of manhattan, he almost spit up and his eyebrows leaped up. It burned.

"You just sip it," his mom said, observing them both from her chair. "Little sips. A long afternoon of little sips."

Kit smiled over at her but set his drink down on the table. Meanwhile, Alice inspected hers as some foreign object floating in it caught her eye. She raised her glass to the dim light to inspect the bottom.

"That's a cherry," Kit's mom told her. "It's real. You can eat it if you like."

Keeping a neutral expression, Alice merely listened,

not trusting herself to speak. The woman stared into her own drink.

"I prefer to save mine 'til the end. But you can eat it anytime."

Her tone had gone back to the dreamy, fairylike quality that she had when she had first greeted them in her garden. The way she spoke so sweetly unnerved Alice, particularly after she'd seen the flip side of Laura's personality. Following Kit's lead, Alice also set her glass down. In a flash, Alice saw what it would be like to live here, where the roles would be reversed. Kit would be the one taking care of his mother, and then who would take care of Kit? From the kitchen, the phone rang. Laura stiffened then anxiously glanced back toward the trilling sound. Instead of making a move to answer the phone, she took a little sip from her drink and eyed them over her glass. Although Kit had gone back to watching the parade, Alice took it as a cue to leave.

"Do you want some ice cream?" she asked Kit.

"No!" he said, as if he was too grown up for such things.

"Yes! Yes!" His mom lit up at the idea. "You kids go get some ice-cream cones. I have some money."

"No, I have money," Kit told her.

"It's a perfect idea," she encouraged.

"Let's go." Alice got up, not wanting to linger.

"Go get ice-cream cones and have some . . . fun."

Reluctantly, Kit followed Alice. On the way out of the room, his mom touched his arm and he clasped hers back instinctually before leaving. They'd only just gotten there and Kit didn't want to part ways for even a moment. But his mom seemed pleased with the idea, so he obliged. He didn't want their rocky start to give her any reason to take back her invitation for him to live with her.

Laura continued rocking gently in her chair, the phone's ringing eventually stopping. As a treat for herself, she fished out the cherry from the bottom of her glass, fingers dripping with alcohol, and popped it into her mouth, chewing slowly and savouring the sweetness.

# AMERICAN PIE

Standing outside the mall, Kit and Alice leaned against the concrete wall of the steps that led up to an employee door. She had brought her camera with her just in case anything worthy of being her last shot caught her eye, and placed it on the landing behind her so she could light a cigarette. Meanwhile, Kit held out his right foot to examine the damage done to his platform shoes.

She couldn't figure out why they were here—why Kit thought that he'd be better off living with his mom. It wasn't even that the woman was weird. Weird she could live with. Everyone was a little bit weird in their own way. Kit's mom was unstable, that much was clear. No matter how much he adored her, Kit couldn't stay with his mom. At her very core, Alice knew it was unsafe. And why he couldn't see it was beyond her.

"What's wrong with your dad?" she asked.

"What's wrong with him?" he repeated.

To clarify she rephrased her question. "Why's he so bad?"

Kit glanced across the parking lot at some distant point. Everyone thought his dad was cool. When cool people said things, others listened. And that was dangerous.

"He doesn't like gay people."

Alice couldn't hide her surprise.

"Did he say that?"

Mr. Morash was so laid back. Granted, he was high most of the time she was over, but he didn't strike her as someone who'd be hung up about that sort of thing. Even Kit's grandmother was kind of hip to things, and not just because she dressed in clothes that women her age usually considered too young.

"He calls people 'fag,'" Kit told her.

"Who?" Alice pressed, wanting specific details to prove that he'd used the ugly word.

"Mr. Bates."

"The French teacher?"

"Yeah."

"To his face?"

"No," Kit started.

The memory of that moment was branded in Kit's mind. His dad was ordinarily pretty mellow, but that night he'd come home in a mood. Kit could always tell when he'd had a bad day because he'd drink a few beers after supper; pot was mostly for weekends. As he did every Wednesday night, Kit had gone downstairs in advance of his grandmother asking him to help prepare the Jiffy Pop. That's when he'd heard his dad spit the word out.

"He was on the phone with someone."

She shrugged it off. "As a joke."

When she passed the smoke to him, he took it and told her, "It's not a joke."

"It just means he's a pain in the arse," she explained.

He took a drag. "Then say he's a pain in the arse."

"It's just a word," she insisted, taking the smoke back. "Everybody says it."

There were lots of words that were used to mean other things. Some of them weren't very nice but people used them anyway. Kit knew that and could think of words that Alice wouldn't like being called. It was a weak excuse. Besides, he couldn't ever remember her calling anyone a fag.

"Do you?"

After considering it, she replied, "No."

He hadn't thought so. Dragging his heels on the asphalt beneath his feet, he started walking away. "Let's get out of here."

Slowly crushing the cigarette under her runner, Alice followed, but doubled back to grab her camera. They made their way back to his mom's house, not saying much of anything. Meandering back though the tangled garden, they entered through the kitchen and into the living room where an Asian man sat at the end of the couch, elbow propped on the armrest and hand on shaved head. A towel was slung over his bare shoulders and shirtless torso. He didn't look like a Jim or an Alejandro—the names of the roommates—so they stared in awe at the man as the bicentennial coverage continued on the television.

"*We've met here today, the fourth of July, to reaffirm our Declaration of Independence and to recommit ourselves to its promise to our country. All across America . . .*"

"Hello?" was all Alice could manage.

"This is my house," the man informed them.

"What?" Kit asked.

His mom came through the doorway from behind, pushing by with another manhattan gingerly cupped in her hands. "This is Mr. Po."

"This is my house," he repeated in answer to Kit's question.

"He's my landlord. And my good . . ." Laura paused. ". . . friend."

She stood at other end of the couch, having deposited the manhattan in front of the man. Clapping her hands together she asked the two of them, "Do you want a fancy drink?"

"No," Mr. Po said to her. "Give them pop. I bring pop."

In the other room the phone rang again. Flustered, Kit's mom promptly made her exit as Alice rubbed her arm anxiously. On her way by, Laura grabbed Alice by the shoulders and pretended to shake her, smiling like it was funny.

For a very long time they stood by the doorway wondering what to do. Eventually, the phone stopped ringing, but not because anyone answered it. Kit's mom whisked back into the room with bottles of pop for the kids, which she handed to them before perching on the arm at the far end of the couch.

She smoked another cigarette while Kit and Alice arranged themselves on the remaining chairs in the room. Everyone had their eyes on the TV except for Alice, who still had her camera out.

Playing with it, she stared at Mr. Po, who sat with one leg crossed, ankle on thigh. He might as well have been a large blue caterpillar sitting on a mushroom smoking a hookah, he was so out of place.

"Can I take your picture?"

Kit's mom got down from her perch and moved to pose next to the man. "Let's get a picture of everybody."

"Can . . . I just take a picture of you?" Alice asked, directing her question to Mr. Po.

Kit's mom staggered back, out of the frame that didn't yet exist.

"Why you want my picture?" Mr. Po asked.

"Mr. Po doesn't want his picture taken." Waving her off like a little gnat, Kit's mom settled back onto the arm of the couch.

Kit glared at his mom from across the room but she was too oblivious to notice. A cloud of smoke billowed around her as she continued to watch the parade. Meanwhile, Alice fiddled with her camera, more interested in the strange man in their midst than what was on the television. So many questions brimmed in her mind until finally one spilled out.

"Are you Chinese?"

"He's from Cambodia," the woman answered for him.

"You know Kampuchea?" Mr. Po asked.

"No," Kit answered from his perch, bolt upright in the wood chair.

Alice leaned forward with interest. "There was a war."

"There is a war," the man corrected. "Yeah. You know Khmer Rouge?"

"No." Alice shook her head.

"Too busy with 'Happy Birthday,'" Mr. Po noted with anger, gesturing to the television. "Happy Birthday America. Why do you care about this people? You are not this people."

With that, he took his drink and departed their company.

"Mr. Po is grumpy today," Kit's mom whispered conspiratorially.

"Who is he, exactly, Mom?"

Kit moved to sit on the couch and his mother joined him.

"He's my landlord," she repeated from before. "And my very good friend."

"Why doesn't he have a shirt on?"

Struggling with an answer she explained, "It's . . . a really hot day. You can take your shirt off if you like."

The idea made Kit uncomfortable. Like an embarrassed child he told her, "I don't want to take my shirt off."

With that, she put out her cigarette in the ashtray and commenced tickling him. "My uptight little prince."

He laughed. "Mom! Stop! Mom!"

When he collapsed on the cushions, she pounced on top of him, fingers digging under his arms to unleash squeals of laughter. Meanwhile, Alice wandered off to talk to Mr. Po about a war that was the furthest thing from their minds.

By the back porch, Mr. Po sat by a glass-topped bistro table in a shaded area of the garden where paving stones had been laid out. Like everything else about the place,

it was overgrown and a bit run down. Dirt and dead
foliage threatened to swallow up the stones and reclaim
that patch of garden. Behind him, a claw-foot cast-iron
bathtub overflowed with a shrub. Beside it was a metal
garbage can with its lid askew.

Mr. Po stared at the fenced in yard, hands clutching
the front of his calf while his ankle crossed over his thigh
again. Still shirtless with only a towel over his shoulders,
the man wore khaki slacks with a braided leather belt and
matching dress shoes. His eyes darted toward Alice when
she appeared, but otherwise he didn't move.

On the table, his manhattan was almost done and he
had an empty pack of cigarettes left open beside an ashtray. She tried to play it cool upon exiting the kitchen,
swinging her arms by her sides and strolling casually onto
the porch. Even though he had the physique of a lion,
something about the way he nervously eyed her made it
seem like he was the prey.

His presence was an unexpected surprise and Alice
wanted to know more about him. Not just because she
was tired of watching the parade or because she wanted
to give Kit time with his mom before she finally convinced
him to leave. All she knew about Cambodia was what
she'd seen on television and in text books. The words and
images only told surface details. If she was being honest, she only ever paid half attention to any of it. Wars

happened on the other side of the world. She probably wouldn't even be able to point Cambodia out on a map.

Not wanting to make her intent obvious, she wandered to the other side of the patio where a ladder was inexplicably tied to a tree trunk at the edge of the wood deck. Beyond that, dozens of plastic milk crates were stacked between two of the garden-fence posts. All things considered, the place was kind of a dive. Of course, Mr. Po had escaped from a wartorn country, so she couldn't blame him for the state of the house. It was probably a far cry from what he'd left behind. Besides, according to Kit's mom, he was just the landlord. So it was his tenants who were being awful about maintaining the place.

Alice rummaged through the eight-track cassettes by the boom box, not really looking at them but stealing covert glances over at Mr. Po, and the stack clattered, tumbling from its pile. When she looked down at the tapes, something out of place caught her eye, and Alice picked up a plastic case for a cassette.

Working up the courage to finally talk to Mr. Po again, she walked over. He watched her every step as she sat in the empty chair across from him. The clear plastic case was filled with cigarettes and she took one out before placing it on the table and sliding it toward him.

"You want a cigarette?" she asked.

Mr. Po picked one up and placed it between his lips.

Sitting at the bistro set on the stone patio made her think of what she'd seen of Paris. The shade could have been from the Eiffel Tower and not a Nova Scotia maple tree. New York was Kit's dream; Paris was Alice's. That was part of why French class had been so important to her, besides bringing her closer to Kit.

Alice crossed her legs as Mr. Po reached out, cupping his hands around the lighter he'd picked up from the tabletop. It was like a scene out of *Casablanca*. There was a war in that movie, too. She leaned forward to accept the light before he lit his own cigarette. As she watched him, it occurred to her that Cambodia was a French protectorate. Or maybe that was Vietnam.

"What's your war about?" she asked.

"Not my war," he corrected. "Kampuchea. You say Cambodia. Near Vietnam. America blow up the border."

A pained expression came over his face. Creases lined his forehead like three frowns, one atop the other. They had learned about the Vietnam War in school. She'd also heard of draft dodgers who had come up from the United States. But she couldn't remember anything about the war in Cambodia except maybe that it had something to do with communists.

"You know?" he pressed.

"No."

"No," he repeated. "You don't know much."

"I guess."

"Stop watching parades," Mr. Po told her. "Is not your parade. You are not this people."

She didn't follow. "Who's 'this people'?"

"Ask Khmer Rouge."

None of what he was saying made sense to her. "Who's Khmer Rouge?"

Mr. Po let out an unexpected little laugh and stood up again. For a moment, she thought she'd said something to upset him again, and in a way she had. It was just like what had happened last night. Everything she thought she knew was wrong. No, she didn't know anything, not really. Maybe she needed to find her escape, like Kit.

Standing with his back facing her, the man removed the towel from his shoulders and spit out the words, "This Khmer Rouge."

Her eyes travelled down his muscled back, down past the dragon tattoo between his shoulder blades to a series of long scars across the back of his ribs to the right of his spine. The raised white tissue intersected in an ugly pattern that spoke of torture. Although the wounds were long healed, physically at least, the scars would be there forever. Suddenly, Alice realized she had no sweet clue what it was like to be unlucky.

With his head titled back slightly and a sneer on his lips, Mr. Po asked, "You want to take my picture now?"

He took a puff of his cigarette.

"Take my handsome picture," he insisted, placing the smoke between his lips and adding, "Cheese!"

Not knowing what else to do, Alice obliged and lifted her camera. Taking the time to frame the picture, she angled the Instamatic so he was off centre from the torso up. The way his shaved head was turned down in the sunlight masked part of his face in shadows. Smoke billowed up from the lit cigarette.

Before she used the last exposure on her roll of film, she took a moment to remember all the details outside of the lens. It was a beautiful day. The clear, blue sky allowed the warmth of the sun to stream down on them. Birds chirped in the trees. The scent of freshly mown grass from a neighbour's lawn wafted over the fence.

Alice lived in a free country where there were no wars, no torture, no crimes against humanity. In that moment, she promised herself she wouldn't take any of it for granted. Then she pressed down. However the photo came out, Alice knew the image would be forever emblazoned in her mind.

# ALL BY MYSELF

**M**r. Po went back inside, not saying anything else after hearing the shutter click on Alice's camera. For a long while, she sat at the table thinking about what it would be like to leave everything behind—to be forced out, not just of one's own house, but one's entire country. She knew that was how Kit felt in a way. But he could always go back home. Mr. Morash would come around once he knew why his son had left in the first place.

When Alice returned to the living room, Kit and his mom were still watching the parade. Nothing had changed since she'd left the room, yet everything had changed. As she slunk into the rocking chair by the door, the glow of the TV cast a pallor on their faces that reminded her of the ghouls from *Night of the Living Dead*. Both stared off mindlessly, seeming to hunger for a different life.

While a marching band on the television played "The Liberty Bell" by John Philip Sousa, crowds of people cheered from the sidelines. Kit's mom joined in the chorus, like any of it mattered to her or any of them for that matter. It was all so surreal.

The woman couldn't be helped, at least not by two teens who were still trying to sort out their own lives, but Alice was determined not to leave Kit in the care of his mom, who was clearly unstable. What he needed was to get out of here so he could get back to living, even if parts of his life were ugly. Alice knew all too well that people didn't get to pick their parents, but at least Mr. Morash had two feet firmly planted in reality.

When Alice let out a frustrated sigh, she regretted it immediately as the sound caught the attention of Kit's mom, who stared past her, at first perking up with anticipation then quickly deflating with disappointment. Mr. Po was nowhere to be seen and Alice could sense a fuse had been lit on a powder keg.

Leaning back on the couch, Kit watched the American Bicentennial but his heart wasn't fully in it. When Alice had left the room, he hadn't pressed his mom about Mr. Po because he hadn't wanted to upset her again, but the man's unexpected presence threw Kit off. There was something she wasn't telling him. His mom had clapped, completely spellbound by the parade, and in a way, it was a small blessing to have the distraction. After the drama with Alice earlier that afternoon, he wasn't sure how he would handle another outburst. But when Alice returned, the magic of the parade was broken, and his mom kept playing with strap of her gown, looking over at Alice by the door, anxious. And when she went to take a sip of her drink she wound up swigging it all back.

He was almost certain that if everyone would just leave, he'd be able to talk to his mom and figure everything out. And if he couldn't, well, he didn't want to think about that possibility.

Mr. Po, having put on a short-sleeved dress shirt, and now slipping into a suit jacket, entered the room then. He stood by the TV and before he could say a word of goodbye, Kit's mom started in on him.

"Where are you going?" she asked in alarm.

"Going." He jutted his chin toward the exit.

"Why do you come if you're just going to leave?"

Her voice was manic again, an unwarranted panic taking hold of her as she rose to walk over to the man.

"Don't get crazy," Mr. Po said softly.

Furious, she gestured wildly, like she was shooing away a stray animal. "Go, then. Go! Go!"

She turned as if to storm off, but was cornered by the bookshelf. Touching the back of her head, she spun back around—it was she who had become the cornered animal.

"Don't get crazy," Mr. Po repeated, even quieter than before.

"Then don't go!"

Kit's mom was almost crying as she pleaded. Alice hugged herself as she watched the events unfold and the woman's sanity unravel. She glanced over at Kit, also watching with concern, clutching a throw pillow to his side. They were both at once horrified and mesmerized.

"I come back tomorrow," the man started to assure her. "Or next day."

Through jagged sobs she railed at him. "Don't come at all if you're going to leave! Don't . . . come back . . . at *all*!"

With that, she picked up a pillow and hurled it at his feet.

"This is my house," he reminded her.

"Go!"

Taking control of the situation, Mr. Po stepped forward. Although he didn't touch her, didn't lay a hand on her, she went still.

"Outside," he commanded. "You come outside. Now."

Alice sat forward, tense. With authority, Mr. Po put his hand around the woman's waist, effectively putting an end to her tantrum. Pouting like a little girl, she was ushered outside. On television, the parade coverage continued and "Hail to the Chief" came on in the background for the president's address.

When the adults were well out of earshot, Alice looked

over at Kit, who was a portrait of misery. All the same, someone had to tell him he couldn't live there.

A door slammed and Kit's mom burst back into the house, crying. They heard her run up the stairs, footsteps thumping. Kit's eyes followed the sound. The momentum of his mother's flight brought him to his feet and up the same steps. Alice opened her mouth to say something more, but decided against it. Instead, she listened to his platform shoes clap upstairs.

When Kit found his mom in her room, she was already throwing things into a suitcase spread open on her bed, pulling random articles of clothing from her closet and tossing them in without folding.

"I'm going away," she announced, voice damp with tears.

"Where?" he asked, perplexed.

"Going away," she repeated, hands spread out on either side of her. In a flurry, she threw on a coat with a fur collar. "To Toronto."

"Toronto?"

It had been years since she'd lived in the city.

"I was happy when I was there." She began buttoning up the coat despite the July heat. "It's a real city. I'll take the bus. I have a bus schedule."

"To Toronto?"

There was no bus to Toronto. Of that he was certain.

"I'll get a job."

"Doing what?"

As far as he knew, she was living off his father's alimony payments, and hadn't had a job since she had been a model.

Putting a hand to her sternum she whispered, "I have money."

"Mom, you don't make any sense, okay?" Kit finally told her. "Do you know that? That you don't make any sense?"

That put a stop to everything. His mom took a breath and stilled.

"You asked me to come here," he reminded her. "You told me to come."

Confusion shadowed her face. "For lunch . . ."

"What?"

"I asked you to come for lunch."

"No," he argued, "you asked me to come live with you."

Her expression told him that she had no memory of that, yet when she looked at him, realization seemed to slowly dawn on her as if she knew he was telling the truth. Collapsing on the edge of her bed, she fiddled incessantly with her coat button. Kit sat on a chair across from her. She wouldn't look him in the eye, choosing to stare out the window instead.

"It gets better and then it gets worse," his mom admitted, petting the blanket on top of her bed. She was trying to hold it together, but failing. Her face contorted and her hand patted the bed frantically. "And when it gets worse, it's worse than before."

A deep sorrow whelmed up and she tried to contain the sobbing, which came out in little hiccups. With her free hand, she stroked the fur on her collar while she took deep breaths and exhaled harshly. Kit leaned down in the chair, elbows on knees, and stared at the floor.

Even though he knew about his mom, he really didn't. It had been a long time since he'd seen her, and never like this. Throughout his childhood she was away often, off on this adventure or that. She would disappear for long periods, then come back for shorter spurts of time. His memories of her were tainted because the magic of being with his mom transported him to wonderful places and they lived life like nobody was watching.

But as with all things that were too good to be true, there was a steep price to be paid. As he grew older, Kit eventually came to understand that her absences were often spent spiralling out of control before hitting rock bottom and having to be hospitalized. But those precious moments he had in between he cherished, and carried them with him like treasure.

Downstairs in kitchen, Alice stood with her back

pressed against the counter, arms wrapped around herself. Everything was as they'd left it earlier that afternoon— dirty dishes strewn about the table, the photo album left open. Eventually, the clap of shoes announced someone's arrival and she held herself tighter in case it was Kit's mom.

Alice was determined not to let him stay—a best friend wouldn't allow it. It was a relief when Kit walked into the room. He caught sight of her, stopped short, and stared off, shoulders slumped like he knew it was over. Alice let her arms slide down. Tilting her head at him, at his disappointment, she wrung her hands.

"You really can't stay here."

He knew she was right. But when he turned to pick up the phone to call home, the weight of the receiver was almost too heavy for him to bear alone. Alice stood by him, waiting—whether he could dial the number himself or needed her help, she'd be there for him. Even after what she'd been through this weekend. He was wrong about what he'd supposed earlier; some people could be simultaneously lucky and unlucky.

His mom had been the life raft that he'd clung to, not realizing she couldn't support the both of them. He had to let go. And when he did, Alice was there to throw him a lifesaver.

# DOWN BY THE HENRY MOORE

Dave Morash had been calling his ex-wife for hours without an answer. Having moved the phone to the coffee table in front of him, he sat in the living room on the sofa with the receiver to his ear and a lit cigarette in his other hand. The phone just kept ringing.

Every ring was a what-if that he shut his mind against. What if Kit hadn't made it to Sydney? What if there'd been an accident? What if he had made it to her house, though? Dave wasn't sure what he was more afraid of— that she was going through a bad spell and Kit was suffering through it too embarrassed to call home for help, or that she was experiencing a good spell and he'd lost Kit to her.

For he knew that normal wasn't an option with Laura. If he'd had any hope of her getting better he would have kept trying. At least, that's what he told himself the last time. But invariably, when she was on a high she'd decide to skip her medications. It was a cruel trick of those drugs, that they gave her a sense that everything was right, that somehow she'd overcome. Each time it was enough that she thought she could cut out the very thing that was allowing her to make sense of the world.

When she stopped taking her meds altogether, how she would fall from such great heights. And it would break his heart. Each and every time. He would have done anything to save her from it, only he was forced to acknowledge many years ago that it wasn't his battle to fight—there were invisible demons that haunted her that only she could conquer.

He pressed the phone's earpiece against his forehead, the ringing continuing. How many times had he tried calling today? Never an answer.

He raised his eyes to his mother, standing across the coffee table from him, hand reaching out. He stared at her outstretched hand then acquiesced to her silent request and gave her the receiver. Without hesitation, she hung up the phone.

"He'll call," Mrs. Morash assured him.

Only then did Dave let it go, a puff of smoke finally exhaling through his nostrils.

An hour later, the phone rang.

"Hello?" Dave answered. "Hello, Kit? Kit is that you?"

The sound of his dad's voice was bittersweet. It broke

something in Kit to have to resort to this phone call. This was the man who had raised him mostly on his own, yet he didn't know Kit—didn't know his own son—enough, seemingly hating what Kit was, who he was, without even knowing it. What could Kit say to his father now that he had him on the phone?

Kit had been convinced that his only escape was through his mother. The irony was that she, too, was trapped, lost in the maze of her mind. More lost than he could understand. A long time ago his dad had given up on his mom. What would stop him from giving up on Kit?

So he was silent, too defeated to ask for help. Alice edged her way over to him and he let her take the phone from him.

"Hi, Mr. Morash," she said. "It's Alice."

"Alice!"

He sounded so relieved that she wished Kit was listening.

"Can you come and get us?"

"Yeah," he replied quickly as if he'd been waiting to be asked. "Yes. Where are you?"

"Uh, we're in Sydney."

He didn't even question it. "I'm coming right now."

Before she even hung up the phone, Kit walked to the kitchen table where the photo album lay open. His fingers touched the image of his mother, the one where she looked so lost. Then he flipped the page. What he saw made his lips quiver. He turned away, leaving through the front door.

Alice put down the receiver and went over to the photo album to investigate. The pages were blank; the rest of the book was empty. Flipping back through the album, she didn't see a single picture of Kit or his dad. It was all just Laura, photo-shoot perfect. What a lonely world she lived in.

Alice scanned the kitchen, looking at the mess that had accumulated during the course of the day. Her eyes fell on a jar of cherries. Kit's mom said she liked saving them until the end, but Kit couldn't even finish the manhattan in order to get to his. Alice took two bowls down from the cupboard and poured the cherries into them, then took them outside.

Kit sat on the front stoop. As she juggled the bowls in her hands in order to close the door, he wiped at his eyes. Sitting on the step next to him, Alice handed him a bowl. They sat in silence for the rest of the afternoon, slowly chewing on the syrupy fruit until they could eat no more. There were no words. Alice knew that any reassurances she gave would be meaningless, and that it was a lie to say everything would be all right.

How desperate must Kit have been to get away from his dad if he willingly came running to his mom and her abundance of issues? Kit must have known, on some level at least, that his mother was ill. Maybe not how far gone she was but . . . all those times he said she went away to Toronto, were they just lies to save face?

Sitting by her side, Kit was utterly despondent as reality finally set in. Now that he'd stopped running from the truth, it caught up with him in a hurry. He'd have to face his dad. And he couldn't bear to think what might happen to his mom. Anger rose at his unlucky circumstances and he gripped the ledge of the step tightly with his free hand, not knowing how he'd manage. He felt his knuckles straining from the pressure.

Then Alice's palm covered his hand and that simple gesture completely undid him. His face contorted in anguish until he couldn't bear it any longer. With a gasp, he shut his eyes and let a warm trickle of dampness stream down his cheeks. He eased his grip on the step, letting Alice's fingers slip between his. This time, when Alice squeezed, she gave him a tiny bit of her strength.

When the familiar blue Datsun finally pulled up and parked on other side of street, they were just stabbing at cherries with toothpicks. Mr. Morash sat in the driver's seat, staring over his shoulder at them. Kit swept his hair back nervously as his dad got out of the car and looked for oncoming traffic. He was dressed in a button-down shirt, sleeves rolled up, and a scuffed pair of jeans. At first, he almost put his hands on his hips but thought better of it. With a stern expression, he strode across the street toward them. Kit's focus turned to his remaining bowl of cherries, sticky from sitting out in the sun for hours. The man stopped directly in front of his son. "Get up." He motioned while speaking, his voice hoarse.

Worried, Kit did as he was told. He stood on the first step, hovering slightly over his dad but feeling smaller than ever. His dad stared at him tensely, glancing over at Alice as if only just noticing her.

Dave took a step forward, reaching up with an open palm. Kit flinched but Mr. Morash only took Kit's face in his hand to get a good look at him. His son, his wonderful, kind boy who had run away from home. The one he'd almost lost. His gaze softened and his hand went to the back of Kit's head, sliding down to his shoulder as he stared. Kit couldn't bear it, couldn't bear to look into his father's eyes.

"Where is she?" his dad asked softly.

Words were lost to him, so Kit looked to Alice.

"Upstairs," she guessed.

He moved past Kit, up the front steps, into the house, and all the way up to the third floor. Dave Morash found his ex-wife kneeling on her bed, curled forward on her elbows. She had an open suitcase beside her with clothes haphazardly thrown in and around it.

This scene was one he knew—one he'd lived dozens of times before. She had worked herself up to the point of running away. If only she could. Try though she might, she'd run to the ends of the earth and never escape it. Because that thing that dwelled inside her would always be there wherever she went. It could never be unpacked.

She heard the clap of his footsteps before she saw him. And when she saw him—the man that she had loved and lost so many times she could no longer count—she crawled up on her knees.

"Hi, sweetie," she greeted him.

A hand went to her mouth to stifle a sob. The words were all jumbled in her head wanting to come out. To explain. To make things better. But nothing would come out except tears. She would drown in them, and all the unspoken words, if she couldn't get them out of her.

Both hands clasped the straps of her gown, gliding up and down the silky fabric as she rocked in place. He stepped toward her, holding his hands out to draw her up into his embrace, where she wept inconsolably. Her fingers clung to the fabric at his chest as he held her, his lips pressed against her brow.

He knelt on the bed with her, hushing her softly and pressing gentle kisses on the top of her head. Still trying to get the words out, she pulled back, but only noise came.

Putting his hands on either side of her face he told her, "It's okay."

He held her close while she wept. From the top of the stairs, Kit and Alice stared at the tender, wounded scene.

Neither of them needed to touch their third eye, the moment would be indelibly seared into their memories as the day they each realized that wanting something simply wasn't enough.

# LANDSLIDE

When he saw them at the top of the stairs, Mr. Morash jutted his chin at them, indicating that they should wait elsewhere.

In the brief time that he had been there, Kit's dad had calmed Laura down. Even though he must have seen her like this a thousand times before, he was still so gentle and patient as he waited for her to let it all out.

Alice thought he must be good for Laura, but then she also understood that wasn't enough—that one person being the right fit for someone else didn't make the reverse true. While it was clear that he still loved Laura, Kit came first in his heart. He had driven over two hours, no questions asked, for Kit. And although it was his ex-wife he was consoling, Mr. Morash would be driving back home with his son, not her. Wasn't that enough proof that he loved Kit? That he could see beyond some stupid word?

Descending the stairs they had just climbed, Kit and Alice made their way back into the kitchen. The only thing for them to do was clean up a bit. It was busywork to fill the time. Words were deficient for the sheer size of the struggles being faced in the house, both upstairs and down. While Kit put away his mom's photo album, Alice cleared some of the plates. She saw the phone out of the corner of her eye and figured it was as good a time as any to call her parents and let them know she'd be late coming home.

When she picked up the receiver and put it against her ear she heard Mr. Morash talking to someone. It only took a few seconds for her to piece together some words—doctor, psychiatric, voluntary. Though brief, she understood what it meant.

"Who are you calling?" Kit asked as he brought more dishes to the sink.

She put her hand on the mouthpiece and shook her head as she put the receiver back in its cradle.

"No one," she said. "Just—I thought I heard it ring."

He gave her a funny look. "Let someone who lives here answer it."

"I did," she lied. "I mean . . . someone's on the phone. They must have got it just as it rang."

Shortly afterward, Kit's parents came down the grand staircase. Mr. Morash gingerly ushered Laura into the kitchen while clutching an orange prescription bottle in his other hand. Kit's mom had let her hair fall loose around her shoulders and she had a too-big woolly cardigan on over her gown.

With the knowledge of what she'd accidentally overheard on the phone, Alice sensed a family conversation might happen.

"I'll go get my things," she said, grabbing her camera from the kitchen table on the way out.

At a snail's pace, she wandered back to the front door where she'd left her satchel. Picking it up off the floor, she stowed her Instamatic, closed the clasps, and shouldered both straps. Then she meandered back toward the kitchen, standing in the doorway.

She folded her arms across her chest, more than ready to go, but the Morashes had just settled in. At the table, Kit sat beside his mom while Mr. Morash stood on the other side with his hands pressed against the wood surface, as if it was the only thing keeping him on his feet.

Laura was drinking a glass of water, gulping it loudly, almost choking. She covered her mouth and wiped at her lips with the sleeve of her cardigan. When she was done, Mr. Morash took the glass and the bottle of pills away from her.

Kit rested his arms on the table. After all these years, his memory of his mother turned out to be smoke and

mirrors. He'd been stuck in time like the Hatter in Wonderland. Somehow, he'd fooled himself into thinking he
could escape the truth, but time always found a way
to catch up. Now the clock wound forward so quickly
that he hadn't had the chance to prepare for his mother's
decline over the years since he'd last seen her.

The nuances of her personality that he'd found charm-
ing as a child had morphed into something different,
something manic, something dangerous. And now that
the looking glass had shattered, he had to tread carefully.

His mom let out a sigh and sniffled back what was
left of her tears. After tucking some stray strands of hair
behind her ear, she put her hand on Kit's and rubbed it as
she looked over at him. All he could do was stare down
as her palm moved against the back of his hand and she
wrapped her fingers around his.

"We're going to start spending more time together,"
she promised, nodding and snuffling. "A lot more."

Kit looked away. She'd forget she'd even said that, just
like she had inviting him to live with her. The cracks in her
mind were massive enough that, big or small, her promises would slip through them and disappear into the ether.

Even though he knew it wasn't her fault and that he
couldn't, shouldn't, hold it against her, there was a nag-
ging part of him that was unable to let go of his disappointment in her. He had hung so much of his hopes

on living with her that he had no backup plan for when it fell apart.

"We'll take a little trip, just you and I," she insisted. "Toronto or . . . New York! Yes, New York, New York. The Big Apple! Won't that be lovely?"

Every word was a lie, a little dagger of untruth. He wondered if she even knew it. The thing was, he would have believed her if she'd said it earlier in the day. Next she'd be saying they'd look up Andy Warhol while they were there.

For as long as Kit had been alive, his mother had been running. From herself. From them. Kit didn't want to admit he'd tried to do the same. Instead of coming out to his dad, he'd fled from the terror of it—of being turned away. He thought if he ran away he couldn't be thrown out of his father's house and somehow he'd win against the bigotry.

But unlike his mother, he could at least have a say in his own fate. One way or another, he was resolved to tell his father that he was gay, no matter the consequence. Fifteen years was long enough to hide from the truth.

Continuing to rub his hand, Kit's mother told him, "I'm going to go . . . to the hospital. For . . . a little while."

He glanced at her from the side of his eyes. "Again?"

As a child, his mother's absences had been attributed to her work as a model taking her to far-off cities like

Toronto. For some period of time it was the truth. Then, when she was gone for longer than she was home and he was old enough to understand, he was told she had to go to the hospital.

As his grandmother had put it, "Something isn't right in her head."

Not knowing any better, he had repeated those very words to his mother once. In response, she had called his grandmother a liar who was jealous and lonely and wanted Kit and Kit's dad all to herself. As the years went by, Laura would be hospitalized on and off, until his parents formally separated then divorced. Eventually, Kit and his dad moved in with his grandmother, and Kit grew up never wanting to speak about his mom's illness, despite his dad's best efforts to explain. In truth, Kit hadn't wanted to believe any of it.

"They're going to try something new."

"Again?" he repeated, this time looking at her.

Unable to contain himself any longer, Kit's dad let out a sigh. "We didn't make a nice home for you?" he asked, frustrated. "Your grandmother and I? It was so terrible?"

Kit recalled the conversation his dad had had on the phone in their kitchen in Antigonish, the word ringing in his ears like it was freshly spoken. Anger welled as Kit glared at him.

He hissed the words, "I'm a fag."

Those three syllables caused his dad to freeze. After a moment, the man's expression melted. Horrified, Kit's mom put her hand under his chin, forcing him to look at her.

In a low whisper she told him, "Don't say it like that."

Resisting her, he angled his face back to his dad, sneering. "That's what you call it. That's what you called Mr. Bates. A *fag*. That's what I am. A fag."

With that, Kit got up, scraping his chair across the hardwood floor and noisily tucking it back under the table before turning away and leaving. He walked past Alice who opened her mouth but then couldn't think of anything to say.

"What did you say?" Kit's mom asked, a pained look on her face as she gazed up at her ex-husband.

Mr. Morash stared after Kit, at a loss for words.

"David," Laura called out, garnering his attention. "What did you *say*?"

"I . . . did you know?"

"Does it matter?"

Putting his hands on his hips, Dave contemplated the situation he now found himself in. It was impossible to say when Kit might have overheard him talking about Mr. Bates. He made it a point to be careful about not saying anything about his colleagues in front of Kit. More confounding though was how he didn't know that his own son was gay. What kind of a father was he?

Not getting a response from him, Laura remarked, "I never imagined you to be the sort to tilt at windmills."

Glancing over at her, he was unsure if she was slipping into fantasy again or merely quoting poetry. Even through the tears that made her eyes puffy, the messy pile of hair she'd pulled back haphazardly, and the sweater that was several sizes too big and made her look so small, his heart swelled. She was and would always be the mother of their boy and the love of his life.

"Oh, my white knight," she said in a singsong timbre. "How many years has it been?"

He shook his head, not entirely sure of her meaning and unable to trust his own voice besides.

"Too many," Laura answered. "A lifetime. I shouldn't have let it go this long."

Still sitting at the table, she clutched her hands together, rubbing one of her thumbs against the back of her hand. Finally, she took a deep quivering breath and exhaled slowly. When she spoke again, it was clear and with purpose.

"I release you from my charge, my love. Do you understand? You need to go now and make this right with our boy."

With a nod, Dave blinked back the dampness in his eyes. He scanned the room, noticing Alice peering around the door frame. With a casual gesture he calmly asked her to wait in the car.

Alice stepped slightly into the kitchen to say goodbye, not knowing when or if she'd ever see Kit's mom again. Alice figured just as Kit's dad had carelessly uttered a word that could have had devastating consequences, it was the small kindnesses that could make a difference in a person's life.

She gave a little wave to the woman and said, "Thanks for the sandwiches."

# SUMMER SIDE OF LIFE

It was a long drive home and a quiet one, too. They each had a lot to absorb. Kit and Alice sat next to each other in the back seat of the Datsun listening to the hum of the car as it sped along the highway. After leaving the city of Sydney, they passed only small towns and remote villages. Most of these places were far removed from each other, like the way they felt right now even within the confines of the vehicle.

With every kilometre marker showing the distance to Antigonish, Kit felt his world closing in on him. He no longer had the comfort of an exit plan. That ship had set sail before he even got to port. The only good thing to come of this road trip was that his mother would get treatment. He'd see her again, of that he was certain, but it would never be the same. He couldn't unsee what her illness had done to her—to the memory he had of her. It had tainted everything.

Meanwhile, his dad still hadn't said anything about him being gay. Maybe he was waiting until they were out of ear-shot from Alice. At home his dad could tear into him, cast him away, bring to life all the terrible things that Kit had imagined time and again before he ran away. And what would his grandmother say about the news? She was from a completely different generation, and while Kit loved her, and didn't doubt her love for him, she wouldn't understand.

He wouldn't live a lie, though. That much he knew. Looking into his future, a lavender marriage was not something he'd abide because he'd never again mislead a girl or break her heart. Seeing how much he'd hurt Alice, how he'd almost lost her, he couldn't do that again. Being openly gay, especially in their small town, would have its consequences, but at least the only person he'd be hurting was himself.

Outside, Kit saw only wide expanses of nothingness and tracts of forests that went nowhere, while Alice ran through conversations in her mind that she'd have with him later in private. At the same time, Mr. Morash kept looking back at them in the rear-view mirror.

The initial shock of Kit's announcement, and the harsh accusatory tone of it, had worn off. What settled in its place was a heavy guilt, like an anchor dragging Dave down further and further away from his son. If he didn't set it loose, he'd lose everything.

Finally he summoned the courage to address his mistake. "Peter Bates might be a good French teacher but he's a bit of a jerk. That's all I'm saying."

He shook his head over the misunderstanding that could have cost him dearly. Both kids looked back at him in the rear-view mirror. In Kit's expression, he could see that it wasn't enough, his explanation. Mr. Morash knew now how wrong headed it was of him to have said the word so carelessly. He felt the wrongness of it in his very core, and it tore him apart on the inside to think his apology was too little, too late.

In the mirror Alice gave him a little smile, knowing she'd been right all along. That he'd just used the word to mean pain in the arse. Kit still scowled. He'd travelled an entire day, so much of it on foot, halfway across the province to get away from the word—from the hateful way his father had spit it out that night on the phone.

"I'm just saying I shouldn't have used *that* word," Mr. Morash said. "That's all I'm saying."

Kit didn't respond. It didn't make it right, but it lessened the sting to hear his dad acknowledge the hurtful choice of word. But he wasn't ready to forgive him just yet.

Unable to endure the long silence, the man continued speaking, putting on a light voice through a fog of emotion. "Oh, hello, Mr. Morash. Can you come and get us?"

In alarm, Kit glanced at his father in the mirror when he realized he was talking to himself. He exchanged a worried look with Alice.

"Oh, hello, Alice," his dad answered himself. "Sure, I can come and get you. Where are you?"

Then he put on what was supposed to be her voice again. "Sydney."

In his own voice he repeated, "Sydney?" And then he laughed, tears filling his eyes. "Sydney. Unbelievable."

He wiped his nose, unable to contain his laughter. At first they smiled, amused, but then he didn't stop. He kept looking over his shoulder at them, choking on laughter until he started crying. His own son had run away to goddamn Sydney just to get away from him. And for what? A word. A horrible, ugly word he never should have used in the first place.

The jagged sobs took over his body and he pulled over onto the shoulder of the road beneath an expansive weeping willow. Sobbing, he clutched the steering wheel with one hand. The kids sat in the back seat, helpless to do anything. Kit closed his eyes. He couldn't bear to have both his parents emotionally off balance, and it gave him no pleasure to know that his father was actually torn apart. The last thing he wanted was to be a disappointment, but that's all he'd accomplished lately.

Somewhere deep inside, Kit felt he deserved to be

rejected. He was a weirdo. He didn't fit. Not here, not anywhere. Who would actually love him if they knew about him? Maybe that was why he had clung to Alice and her unwavering love for so long even though he'd suspected the truth well before she came into his life.

Alice sensed what Mr. Morash was going through wasn't quite the same as when Kit's mother had cried. His momentary breakdown came from a place of a father's concern over almost losing his son. It was understandable. But Alice knew he needed to pull it together. After everything they'd been through, what they needed was a sense of normalcy so they'd all know that everything would be okay, even if it wasn't just now.

Dave took deep calming breaths, pressing his eyelids shut in between, until he regained his composure. She waited until there was enough of a pause between sobs that he would hear her.

"Can we get some fries?" she asked.

In the rear-view he looked at her, silent, processing her words.

"You want to get some fries?" he repeated. Then with a shaky voice he asked his son, "You want to get some fries, Kit?"

"Okay," he agreed.

Dave nodded. "Let's get some fries, Alice." He smiled back at her. "Shall we get some fries?"

"Okay."

After one last sniff, he started the car. "Okay."

They drove a ways until they found a burger joint on the side of the highway. It was a little white house with a takeout window on one side. Lettering, like that from a sandwich board, was pasted on the shingles that listed the specials. Kit's dad got them each a box of fries, and they sat outside at a picnic table, Alice on one bench and Dave seated on the tabletop near her. Kit straddled the other bench so he had his back to his dad.

The line cook stood outside on a smoke break, wearing a white apron and paper hat. They ate their fries in silence, each in their own world. The air around them was thick with the smell of grease. But for a moment, there was peace.

Afterward Dave drove them home, stealing glances in the rear-view mirror every once in a while. Clear headed now, his heart was lighter knowing that he had his son back. It would take effort to earn Kit's trust, but it would be well worth it.

Alice fell asleep while Kit took in the scenery. They drove along same highway Kit and Alice had travelled. From the other direction, the sights looked different somehow.

Cape Breton Island had a certain majesty in the untamed beauty of its rocky shorelines and mountainous forests.

Mainland Nova Scotia had rolling fields filled with various crops or cattle. Even though the latter felt small at times to Kit, it also felt like home.

Eventually, he too fell asleep, and when Dave glanced back at them, Kit and Alice were leaning against each other as the sun filled the car. He thought of an old Gaelic blessing his mother had cross-stitched on a wall hanging.

> May the road rise up to meet you. May the wind always be at your back. May the sun shine warm upon your face, and rains fall soft upon your fields.

As much as he dearly wanted to hold Kit in his own hand, his son had all but grown up. If he couldn't shelter Kit from his father's own words, how could he shelter him from the world's? All he could hope for now was to make amends. To try better. And to always hope his son had a friend as good to him as Alice was.

# SNOWBIRD

"**I** like your dad," Alice said.

She and Kit sat on the back steps of his wood deck in the late afternoon. The Datsun was parked by a wood pile at the side of the house. Kit had his hands clasped in front of him, elbows leaning on thighs. Everybody liked Alice, so it was easy for her to like them back. He didn't respond.

"You're lucky."

With a scoff Kit looked out over the rolling fields behind his home and the farmhouse in the distance. As a kid, whenever he came to visit his grandmother he used to wonder how long it would take him to race across the field—how quick he could be. He'd never been brave enough to do it. Now, years later, he was done with running.

When he still didn't say anything, Alice sat up straight, as if to recite a poem or something. "And they walked along the road," she started.

Shutting his eyes against it, Kit knew what she was trying to do. She was trying to make it better, to lift him out
of his funk. But she wouldn't ever fully understand what
he was going through.

In many ways, Alice lived and would live a charmed
life. She thought that she existed in the shadow of her
sister, Denise, who had gone to Halifax to study medicine at Dalhousie. The kids in school and people in town
still fawned over her. They were either living vicariously
through her success or attributing the success to her having lived here back in the day.

It would be the same with Alice, whatever she did in
her life. With Kit though, he'd be talked about in other
ways. Quietly, with hands over mouths, as people whispered conspiratorially among each other, or angrily over
the phone, late at night in a kitchen after one beer too
many. There would be worse, too.

The one place where he was supposed to feel safe and
loved unconditionally had been pulled out from under
him. Kit had never been completely sure footed in his own
skin, and then he was hobbled unexpectedly by his own
father. Now that he'd come out, it was like he was learning how to walk again.

Still Alice persisted. "Walking and walking and walking and walking . . ."

Kit opened his eyes to finish the story. "And the helicopter never came and New York disappeared and there was no party and everything turned to *crap* for everybody."

Alice grimaced. "Maybe we shouldn't move to New York."

It had just been a fantasy anyway. Something they'd said to kill the time. Even if they made it there, New York, or the version of New York that they envisioned, likely didn't exist. Kit wouldn't be able to bear the disappointment of it.

"Maybe we should live in Toronto," she suggested with a broad smile on her face as she recalled an image she'd seen once. "Did you ever see their city hall? It looks like a spaceship."

"I bet Andy Warhol was never even in Toronto," he muttered.

Everything his mother had ever told him was probably a lie. She existed in some sort of made up, make-believe world where everything was perfect except when it wasn't. And when it wasn't, she would just pack up and leave a wake of broken promises behind her.

The truth of the matter was that there had never been any space in her life for Kit. It was already too crowded with people she'd never even met, parties she'd never even gone to. Through all the years that his parents had been living together as a family, it really had only been Kit and his dad in it together.

Alice shrugged, refusing to let him mire himself in

bitterness. "Maybe we can be Andy Warhol in Toronto."

The idea resonated with Kit who turned it over in his mind. Could he do that? Could he be Andy Warhol? Wasn't that what he was doing anyway, carrying on conversations with the man in his head?

The back door opened just then and his grandmother poked her head out. "Did your mother say you could stay for supper, Alice?"

Alice turned to look over her shoulder. "Yeah."

"Could you help me peel the potatoes?"

"Okay."

Before she left, Alice reached out and put her hand on Kit's, squeezing gently before hopping up the steps.

"Disney's coming on soon, Kit," his grandmother noted before shutting the door.

"She's such a sweetie," Andy Warhol observed. He sat in a lawn chair with a camera in his lap, staring off into the field. "I'd love to take her picture."

Kit had to ask, "Were you ever in Toronto?"

"I think so," Andy Warhol replied, unconvincingly. "Maybe. Sure, why not? I like Canada."

For some reason that last statement surprised Kit. "Why do you like Canada?"

"Well, you're all kind of weirdos." Andy Warhol's eyes strayed over to Kit. The man grinned. "Which is a good thing. And your flag is a leaf."

Kit shook his head, not following. "So?"

"It's just a leaf," Andy Warhol repeated, astonished. "It's kind of nice. I like trees. They never steal your stuff. And they never call you at four in the morning looking for money."

The conversation had gone way off course. Kit corrected the direction by asking, "So, what happens now?"

"Whatever's possible."

That brought Kit back all the way to the start of his journey, standing beneath the highway overpass worrying about wrecking his shoes. He looked at the man sitting in the lawn chair and tried to see through him. "Are you really Andy Warhol?"

"Sure, why not?"

Andy Warhol lifted the camera to his eye, squinted, then snapped a picture of Kit. The Polaroid film screeched out the bottom and he lowered the camera so he could stare into Kit's face.

"We're all a little Andy Warhol."

Then he winked.

And then he was gone.

# WELCOME BACK

They ate in the kitchen, twilight casting a golden glow over them through the curtains. Kit's grandmother usually made a traditional hodge-podge for Sunday dinner in the summer. Tonight, though, they had pork chops with applesauce and mashed potatoes. It was no coincidence that it was Kit's favourite meal. There was even blueberry grunt for dessert.

As the radio played in the background, the mealtime conversation turned to their weekend adventure. It was Alice who recounted an edited version of what had transpired, not outright lying, but leaving out details not meant for those who hadn't experienced it first hand. She tried to draw Kit into the conversation, but he would only respond with a nod or noncommittal noise.

"Kit's going to learn to play the piano," she announced.

"Is that right?" his grandmother pressed, ever so interested.

"Yeah," was all he would say on the matter.

So Alice went on to say she had decided to become a police officer. Kit's grandmother was very encouraging about it. There had been much ado about the RCMP accepting female officers into the force only two short years ago. Mrs. Morash told her she'd heard it on CBC Radio.

"The reporter had a clever way of putting it: 'The force that always gets its man now has women.'"

That news made Alice all the more proud of her decision. At the same time, Kit began to realize there were hurdles that she would have to face in a life as a woman in a line of work that was traditionally left to men. And he felt a pang of guilt for so glibly thinking she had it so easy in life.

Alice kept her word to the RCMP officer who'd given them a ride and didn't mention anything about the drunk that had gotten behind the wheel of the cruiser, with them in it, and how he almost crashed into the side of the barn. She figured it was for the best, especially since they'd come out unscathed.

Suddenly, Alice remembered another detail that she recounted with a pleasant smile on her face. "Mr. Morash, we met some kids yesterday who thought you were really cool."

"Really?" he said, equally as quiet as Kit during the meal.

"Mm-hmm."

"Well, that's nice."

She nodded emphatically, eyes wandering over to Kit, who drank a glass of orange juice. He stared over at her, seeing what she was trying to do. Alice was on a mission to fix the broken bridge between him and his father.

"Does that surprise you?" Dave asked.

"No," she answered honestly.

"What about you?"

He turned to his son, who merely shrugged. Sitting kitty corner to Kit, his grandmother had her elbows on the table, cheek against a clenched hand, looking thoroughly invested. The glass of white wine in front of her was practically untouched.

"Does your mother have a nice house?" she inquired.

At the mention of his mother, Kit's lips pursed and he rolled his eyes over to her. "Not really."

She lifted her head away from her hand. "I bet she has a really nice yard, though. Does she have a nice garden?"

"Kind of."

"You should write a story!" she suggested, inspired. "You like writing stories."

"About what?"

Unable to find a way through to Kit, his dad lit a cigarette and disengaged from the conversation.

"About your weekend," Mrs. Morash said.

"Why?" Kit had his tongue thrust inside his cheek, not making eye contact.

His grandmother spoke with a little flourish of her hand. "Because sometimes when you turn something into a story and you can stand a bit outside it, then you can, you know, you can better see your place in it. See where we fit. Does that make sense, David?"

At the mention of his name, Mr. Morash returned to the conversation. "It does."

"Not to me," Kit murmured.

"It does to me," Alice said.

The discussion wavered, dying out despite all efforts to revive it. After a pause, Kit's grandmother found another way in. An unexpected one at that.

"You remember your great uncle Charlie?"

"Not really," Kit replied.

"Mom?" Dave interrupted, sitting forward in his chair.

At his concerned tone she perked up, explaining herself. "He had a dance studio with his friend Bob."

"Mom," he repeated calmly, not sure where she was going with the story.

"I'm just saying Uncle Charlie was a very nice fellow," she assured him.

"I don't really remember him," Kit told them, curiosity peaked.

"Well, he was a lovely fellow," his grandmother

remarked. "He taught your father how to dance."

Dave let out a heavy sigh. With his elbows on the table, he pressed the heels of his palms into his eyes. If she didn't know any better, Alice would say he was embarrassed.

"Mr. Morash dances?" she asked.

"He does." Kit's grandmother had a teasing tone in her voice. "Come on, buddy. He dances."

"Cool." Alice giggled.

"Come on, Dave."

Kit's grandmother went over to the radio perched on top of the fridge and turned it up as his dad sat back in his seat.

"Come on. Show your son how cool you are, Dave."

"What?" he said, feigning ignorance.

"Come on."

Jiggling in her seat, Alice smirked and encouraged him to get up silently.

"Show Kit what Uncle Charlie taught you."

A puff of smoke escaped as he let out a humouring laugh, his expression letting on that he was entertaining the request.

"Come on, Dave. Come on."

He rubbed his eyes, raised his eyebrows in defeat, then nodded. Putting out his cigarette, he got up. Kit's grandmother was already dancing in spot and Kit couldn't help but smile. Then his dad joined his grandmother in a gentle swing dance. At first, he moved with reluctance, but then he got into it.

Kit was embarrassed but had to admit his father had moves. And it was in that moment that he understood that his dad really couldn't have hated his uncle Charlie, whoever he was, if he'd learned to dance with him.

Alice was absolutely delighted, squealing with laughter as the adults danced around the kitchen. She and Kit looked at each other across the table, smiling. Without any hesitation Alice raised two fingers and pressed them to her third eye. It was a perfect moment after such an imperfect weekend.

To capture it forever, Kit did the same. Lucky.

# ABOUT THE AUTHOR

Kat Kruger is Chief Wordsmith at Steampunk Unicorn Studio, specializing in writing for the entertainment and media industries. She is also the young adult author of the Lycan Code series (formerly The Magdeburg Trilogy). As part of her freelance work she teaches creative writing through gamified learning and holds a degree in public relations from Mount Saint Vincent University.